some kind
of PRIDE

OTHER DELL YEARLING BOOKS YOU WILL ENJOY

DELL YEARLING BOOKS are designed especially to entertain and enlighten young people. Patricia Reilly Giff, consultant to this series, received her bachelor's degree from Marymount College and a master's degree in history from St. John's University. She holds a Professional Diploma in Reading and a Doctorate of Humane Letters from Hofstra University. She was a teacher and reading consultant for many years, and is the author of numerous books for young readers.

some kind
of PRIDE

Maria Testa

A Dell Yearling Book

Published by
Dell Yearling
an imprint of
Random House Children's Books
a division of Random House, Inc.
New York

Visit us on the Web! www.randomhouse.com/kids

Educators and librarians, for a variety of teaching tools, visit us at
www.randomhouse.com/teachers

ISBN: 0-440-41669-8

Reprinted by arrangement with Delacorte Press

Printed in the United States of America

March 2003

10 9 8 7 6 5 4 3

OPM

For Ellen,
my best friend

Saturday afternoon
   —pregame practice, Red Hill vs. East Shore

   The game is scheduled to begin in twenty minutes, which means infield practice should be over in about five. My teammates slowly jog off the field, leaving me alone at shortstop. I watch my afternoon shadow loom tall in front of me, and I know that I am bigger than life.

   Coach Jameson steps up to the plate with a bat and a bag of baseballs, ready to begin our pregame ritual. Coach Dillon pounds his glove at first base, smiling and waiting. Suddenly hard, bounding, adult-size grounders are flying at me, one after the other, and I dive to my left and to my right, whipping chest-high strikes to first.

   "Awesome," I hear someone murmur, and I know that people are watching.

   For five minutes nonstop, Coach Jameson pounds ball after ball at me as hard as he can, and I make every play. I am dirty and sweaty and I am the best. Everyone says so.

Coach Jameson runs out of baseballs. He waves me off the field. I flop on the grass near third base and stretch out, relaxing before the game begins. I close my eyes while the sun warms my face, pretending to be far away, but I am listening. The adults are talking.

"Unbelievable," a man's voice says. "That's what I call major-league talent."

Lots of different voices join in, agreeing, and I can't help smiling.

"You must be so proud, Tony," a woman says, and I know that my father has arrived. He's never missed a Little League game since my oldest brother, Joe, first put on a uniform eight years ago. I imagine my father standing in the middle of all the parents, hands in his pockets, rocking back on his heels, a smile spreading across his face.

"All of your kids are good athletes, Tony," another man says, "but this one is something special."

"I know." My father's voice is soft. I strain to hear his every word. "Real major-league talent. But I can't help thinking what a shame it is that it's all wasted on a girl."

Chapter 1

Mama had been dead for eight years the summer I was eleven and the man from *Sports Illustrated* came to Maine and Ellie Sanders became a feminist. All these things seemed important at the same time. I had known that my mother was dead for as long as I could remember, but it wasn't until shortly after my eleventh birthday that I knew I missed her. The man from *Sports Illustrated* meant fame, or something like it, and he had to be important because all the adults said so. And Ellie. Ellie Sanders was my best friend. Everything about Ellie was important.

But I wasn't thinking about any of those things that Sunday in June when Ellie insisted it was warm enough

3

to spend the afternoon at the beach. "Just look at the calendar, Ruth," she said. "It's summer."

So I sat on a blanket on the nearly deserted beach at the end of our street, wearing a blue-and-white-striped one-piece bathing suit, shivering and watching the walkers and clammers and trying not to think about baseball, trying not to think about the day before.

I thought maybe I was supposed to be having fun. I looked at my best friend for a clue. Sure enough, Ellie was having big fun.

First of all, she was wearing a purple bikini and carrying a pink beach pail, both of which totally clashed with her wild-and-curly reddish brown hair. She was so short and skinny she could have almost passed for an elementary school kid, except for the fact that she was actually starting to fill out her bikini top. The stripes on my suit, on the other hand, ran from top to bottom without so much as a bump along the way. But Ellie didn't care about any of that stuff. She'd probably still be playing with pink beach pails when she was eighteen. Ellie just loved summer. She wished it was summer all the time.

I couldn't really blame her. Summers were always pretty wonderful in East Shore but hard, too, somehow. Summers were when people who made their living from the water had to do well, or else. Almost everyone in town fished in some way. Some just liked to hang a line off a boat to see what might happen. Others fished to survive. From what I'd heard, that was the way it had always been, and that was the way most people wanted it to stay. East Shore, Maine, wasn't exactly famous for being on the cutting edge of anything.

As for me, summers were always about baseball and Ellie and the beach. And since I wasn't thinking about baseball, I decided to think about Ellie and the beach.

I watched Ellie leap around me in a blaze of purple and pink. She scooped up sand and poured it onto an enormous mound in front of us so that we could begin constructing a life-size sand castle. Ellie's idea.

I wanted to think about castles.

I gathered up the ends of my blanket and wrapped them around my shoulders as if that would help me stop missing Mama.

The mound of sand in front of me was growing taller, and beads of sweat were actually visible on Ellie's forehead when she stopped jumping around and turned to me.

"I am a feminist," she announced. "I have decided."

I stared at her as if I didn't understand, but I had to admit, it was an Ellie thing to say.

It was the kind of comment Ellie was capable of making anytime, anywhere, even at the worst imaginable time, like when she asked if anyone had gotten her period yet at the exact, horrible moment our sixth-grade girls' gym class at East Shore Middle School was trying to slip out of shorts and T-shirts and back into regular clothes as quickly and anonymously as possible. It was

the kind of comment Ellie would make in an unbeliev-
ably loud voice that would be followed by dead silence
and then someone, anyone, whispering to me accusingly,
"She's *your* best friend."

I was glad we were at the beach. And I was glad we
were alone.

I looked at Ellie. A streak of wet sand swept across
her left cheek, and I knew she probably didn't know
about it and definitely didn't care.

"It's an important decision," she continued. "I'm
really happy with it."

"That's nice," I said. I smiled at Ellie, and then I
waved at Josh Callahan.

He couldn't have chosen a better time to walk by.
Josh was the neighborhood paperboy and my brother
Lou's best friend. He was barefoot, wearing khaki pants
rolled up to his knees and a white long-sleeve T-shirt,
and he was fifteen and sandy-haired and perfect. He
stopped and eyed our pile of sand.

"Cool dune," he said to Ellie, somehow knowing it
was her creation. Then he turned to me and held out his
hand, waiting for me to slap it. "Great game yesterday,
Ruthie."

I slapped Josh's hand hard because he expected me
to. He groaned and smiled as I expected him to. My relationship with Josh was nothing if not consistent.

"You know, Ruth," he said, "I hate to give out free
advice, but—"

"You love it," I cut in.

"Okay," he admitted, still smiling. "But I couldn't help noticing that in the fourth inning yesterday you let Cal Landry make a play that should have been yours."

I remembered that play well. I couldn't forget it. Every play, every moment from that entire game had been haunting me since the final out.

"Maybe," I said. "I'll think about it."

"But you still had a great game," Josh said, holding out his hand a second time. I dutifully slapped it, more lightly this time.

Ellie watched him walk away.

"He's beautiful," she practically whispered. I was afraid she might faint.

"And you're eleven," I said. "Some feminist."

Ellie scooped up more sand in her pail. "Feminists are allowed to like boys," she explained. "We just can't let them know it."

I watched Ellie work. I knew I should have been helping, but I also knew that I could never gather sand quite as well as Ellie. She was so weird and beachy and happy. *Happy*. I didn't know if I could ever be happy like Ellie, even during the summer. Even on the beach.

She sprawled beside me on her blanket, gazing up at the pile of sand.

"It's absolutely magnificent," she announced. "There's no need to turn this marvelous creation into a castle—it's perfect the way it is."

"You're tired," I said.

Ellie smiled. "My mother says feminists don't have time to be tired. Our work is never done."

I looked at the sandpile. I didn't see anything marvelous or magnificent. A castle was something to be.

"Hey, Ellie," I said suddenly, the tone of my voice issuing a challenge I had not intended. "What would you say if someone told you that you really weren't all that creative a person, that maybe you're kind of a fake? I don't know. Like maybe you should give up on the whole idea of art school and go work in a bank or something."

Ellie just stared at me.

"I mean," I continued, "what exactly would you say if someone said something like that?"

"Who said that about me?" Ellie's eyes narrowed. "You might as well tell me, Ruth, because I could probably figure it out, you know."

I felt bad immediately. I could probably have figured it out, too, if I hadn't just made it all up. Ellie Sanders had been voted the "Most Creative" sixth grader in school at the end of the year, but there were a lot of kids who thought "Most Creative" was just another way of saying "Weirdest."

"Nobody said anything, Ellie," I said. "I'm just making it up, asking 'what if?' . . ."

Ellie looked at me, and then at her sandpile, and then at me again. A gull called in the skies above us, and I craned my neck, shielding my eyes with my hand, searching.

"I'd tell them," Ellie said, "that I am going to be the most famous feminist performance artist to play Carnegie Hall. Just like you're going to be the first woman shortstop to start in the Major League All-Star Game. Right?"

"Right," I said softly. "Sure. But you're lucky, Ellie. You're so clear about everything. You're lucky you know what you are."

Ellie looked surprised. She smiled as if she was pleased with what I'd said. "And you're lucky, too, Ruth," she said, "because you know what you love."

I had to turn away. I couldn't tell Ellie that she was wrong. I couldn't tell Ellie that my talent, my love, was all a waste. How could I possibly love something that was wasted on me?

"What I love?" I asked, watching the waves grow stronger with the incoming tide. "What do I love?"

"Baseball," Ellie stated, as if it was a fact. "You love to play baseball."

I dropped my blanket and jumped to my feet, gathering sand in my hands to add to Ellie's dune that would never be a castle. *What a shame.*

"Used to," I said. "Used to love to play baseball."

Chapter 2

I had always loved to play baseball. It was how I measured everything in my life. How sick was I? Too sick to go to school? Maybe. Too sick to play baseball? Never. How tired was I? Too tired to play baseball? Impossible. Too busy to play baseball? Too busy to do anything else. Baseball was like air in my family. We lived on it from the moment we were born.

Dad claimed that Mama shared his love of baseball. He said that when my brother Joe was born seventeen years earlier, Mama agreed completely that he had to be called Joseph Paul DiMarco, which is about as close to Joseph Paul DiMaggio as you can get. And when Lou was born two years later, she had absolutely no objection to naming her second son Henry Louis in honor of Dad's second-favorite New York Yankee, Lou Gehrig.

But four years later, Mama drew the line at naming her only daughter George Herman. It was in the spirit of loving compromise, according to Dad, that Mama agreed to acknowledge the greatest baseball player of all time, and I came to be called Ruth. Ruth Sofia, that is, because Mama believed the name Sofia was both classy and beautiful. My middle name was the one thing about me that I knew for sure came from my mother.

"It's the Babe," Dad greeted me as I arrived home from the beach, covered in sand. In a fit of inspiration, Ellie, my completely nonathletic, feminist best friend, had successfully pushed me, the superstar, into the world's biggest sandpile. I had become one with the sand, and I was squeamish at the thought of looking inside my bathing suit. My itchy bathing suit. I could only imagine where most of the sand must have settled.

Dad sat at our dining room table, which wasn't really a dining room table, since it was in the living room and we had never in our lives dined at it. The table was actually home to Dad's computer and his books and his files and everything else he needed to write his syndicated sports column. Dad's articles appeared in newspapers throughout the country, and they were all created right on our dining room table. People in New York and Los Angeles and everywhere else read Dad's stuff all the time. It was kind of a cool thing to think about, even though our living room was always a mess.

Dad watched me contribute to that mess, tracking sand across the wood floor and onto the rug.

"Joe'll get it," I said, because it was Joe's job to vacuum every Sunday night, and I knew Dad didn't really care.

I stood behind him, peering over his shoulder at the computer screen. "What're you working on?"

"It's an article—a retrospective, really—about Mickey Mantle," Dad said. "Do you want to read what I've got so far?"

I didn't. I also didn't know what to say. Maybe: No, Dad, I don't want to read about a hero I can never really have. Or how about: Sorry, Dad, but I'm too busy wasting all this talent your sons could have had.

But I knew I could never say anything like that to Dad. Before the Red Hill game, I would never even have *thought* about saying anything like that to Dad. As it was, I didn't want to talk about baseball with anybody. And if I couldn't talk about baseball with my father, that didn't exactly leave us with a lot of topics for conversation. Baseball had always made our relationship simple and easy. And that was the way we liked it.

"That's okay," I said. "I'll read it when you're done."

"Good enough." Dad gave me a quick hug. "You need a shower. Or maybe you should just go put the beach back where you found it," he teased, making me smile.

"I'll go shower now," I said. I started up the stairs, leaving sandy footprints behind me. For Joe.

"Hey, Babe," Dad called after me. "Nervous about tomorrow?"

I heard myself take a deep breath. Tomorrow would be all about baseball. "I'm trying not to think about it," I said.

"Just be yourself and you'll be fine," Dad said. He shook his head. "I can't believe my little Face in the Crowd is already moving to the feature pages of *Sports Illustrated*. What you're doing is pretty special, you know, especially in this town. Your mother would have been so proud."

"As proud as you, Dad?" I couldn't help asking, although I knew I was on the verge of breaking our simple and easy rule.

Dad smiled. "At least," he said. "And you know, Babe, I couldn't be more proud of both of my groundbreaking women."

I waited for him to say more, but he had already turned back to his computer. Dad never talked much about Mama. He would answer our questions, but in order to have questions answered, you needed to ask. I rarely asked. It always seemed as if Dad preferred it that way.

I dashed up the stairs and into the bathroom, closing the door behind me while tearing off my bathing suit, practically in one motion. Sand poured off me. I still itched all over.

I stepped into the shower and finally allowed myself to really think about the next day. A man from *Sports Illustrated* was coming to write a feature article about me, the little girl from nowhere on the coast of Maine who could play baseball better than any of the boys.

A year before, I had been a Face in the Crowd, one of those people whose picture appears in the beginning of the magazine with a short blurb about how many home runs they hit or whatever. My blurb had been longer than anyone else's on the page, packed with statistics and awards. But it didn't say anything about how much I loved baseball. It didn't say anything about pride.

So Dad said Mama would have been proud. I watched the sand run off my body and turn into mud as it disappeared down the drain. I tried to hear Mama telling me she was proud, but I did not know her voice.

I could hear Dad telling me he was proud, though. Joe and Lou, too, sometimes. I knew their voices well.

"And what about you?" I asked out loud, not knowing who I expected to answer. It occurred to me for the first time in my life that it would have been nice to have a little sister named Mickey.

Late that night I lay in my bed, staring into the darkness. Maybe I was nervous. Maybe I was wondering if I was a feminist. Maybe I should have read Dad's Mickey Mantle article. Maybe I was thinking about Mama. What had Dad said? *My two groundbreaking women.* But he had said other words, too; words I wished I had not heard.

Suddenly I was on my knees reaching under the bed, pulling out the two scrapbooks Dad had given to me. One was a collection of articles about Mama, about being the first woman firefighter in East Shore, about dying when that roof collapsed, about being a hero. The second scrapbook was all about me and everything I had ever done on the baseball field, about being more than a face in the crowd.

I sat there on the floor in the dark, caressing the two scrapbooks, the most valuable things I owned, wondering why mine was already thicker.

Saturday afternoon
   —top of the 1st, bases empty, 1 out, Red Hill 0, East Shore 0

I'm standing at shortstop, making circles in the dirt with my toe, wondering why I'm feeling so cold, even numb, standing here in the afternoon sun, when from somewhere I hear the ping of a ball slicing off a bat, and then suddenly there's this baseball coming straight at me like it's going to eat me up alive, and I take a step backward—which is the worst thing a shortstop can do—and with my bare hand stab at the ball somewhere around my right ear and in one motion fling it to first base just in time to hear the umpire yell "Out!" at the top of his lungs, making me wonder why he can't be just a little quieter about it. Some people are trying not to think.

Cal Landry comes scooting over to me from second

base, and he's giggling like a two-year-old. He swats me on the back of the head with his glove.

"Wake up, man," he says. "You just made a great play on a routine ground ball."

"I'm fine," I tell him. "You worry about second base. I've got everything covered over here."

I glance over at the dugout and Coach Jameson is smiling and shaking his head.

I look behind the dugout where the parents are sitting and see my father, laughing and proud. Someone slaps him a high five, and I imagine I can hear what they are saying, or maybe I really do: "She's so good, your daughter, she just can't screw up, not even in her sleep."

I kick at the dirt around me with both feet. I'm making holes, I think, not circles but holes big enough to stand in, up to my ankles, up to my knees, holes so big I can't get out of them, and then, no matter what happens, no matter what I am, I will always be where I belong.

Chapter 3

Something was up with my brothers.

Early Monday morning I heard them clanging around in the kitchen, and then the aroma of French toast with cinnamon apples, my favorite breakfast, drifted up the stairs.

"Hey, superstar," Lou called out. "Breakfast is ready for anybody who's going to be in *Sports Illustrated*."

My brothers worshiped *Sports Illustrated*. Random issues were strewn about the house. Not-so-random covers were clipped and saved and sometimes tacked on walls.

I staggered downstairs, still in the sweatpants and T-shirt I had worn to bed. I knew I was a mess. And I was sure my hair was standing straight up, too. My hair was trouble. It was thick and black with a life of its own and looked best stuffed into a baseball cap. It was the family hair, actually; we all had it. Only I had the girl version, which meant more of it. As a rule, I tried to avoid mirrors first thing in the morning.

I practically ran toward the kitchen. I wanted to ride this wave of attention from Joe and Lou as long as possible. During normal times, like when I wasn't about to be interviewed by *Sports Illustrated,* my brothers did not live in my world. At most, they came for the occasional visit, usually when I was on the baseball field. But French toast with cinnamon apples? I recognized something special when I saw it.

I slid into the kitchen on bare feet, a grand entrance.

"Nice hair" was the first thing Lou said to me.

"You mean, 'Nice hair, superstar,' " Joe added.

He pulled out my chair while Lou placed a plate of French toast on the kitchen table. They hovered around me.

I took the first bite.

"Good?" Joe asked.

"Great," I answered, before I had really tasted it. I would have said it was great if it had tasted like rubber.

"Cool," Joe said, and two more plates suddenly appeared on the table as my brothers sat down beside me. I couldn't remember the last time the three of us had eaten breakfast together.

I took another bite. Joe watched me, smiling.

"What is it?" I asked, suddenly self-conscious. "You're not going to just sit there and watch me eat, are you?"

"This is a big day, Ruthie baby, and it's going to be a great week," Joe said. "Lou and me, we'll stay out of your way, but if there's anything we can do to help—"

"Oh, great," Lou interrupted. "Reduced to the role of groupies by our baby sister."

Joe rolled his eyes, still smiling. "Jealous," he whispered loudly, pointing at Lou.

"Big-time jealous," Lou said. "Chopped-liver jealous. Minor-league jealous."

Joe laughed. "That's right, Lou, minor-league. That's where you'll be spending your career."

"Uh-huh." Lou nodded in exaggerated agreement. "And that's where I'll be catching your not-quite-major-league-caliber fastball."

I watched my brothers slap hands and grin at each other as if I had suddenly disappeared. That was the way it had always been, for as long as I could remember. They were their own unit, on the field and off: Joe a pitcher, Lou a catcher, and no need for anyone else.

"So, what time are we expecting this *Sports Illustrated* guy, anyway?" Lou asked. "You think he's going to call before he shows up?"

"Dad doesn't know for sure," Joe answered. "He said he doesn't know any details, just that the guy is flying into Portland, renting a car, and driving up the coast sometime this morning. I think he's staying with friends at a summer house not far from here. Dad said something about this sort of being a vacation for him, too."

Lou tipped his chair back and drummed his fingers on the table. "I can't stand this," he said. "What am I so uptight about? It's not like he wants to talk to me."

"He might want to talk to you guys, too," I suggested. "I mean, you're both really good baseball players. He's probably going to want to talk to the whole family. He must know who Dad is, right?" I smiled. I felt pretty good about offering to share my *Sports Illustrated* interview with my two older brothers.

Joe and Lou glanced at each other quickly, but I saw it. I suddenly had the feeling that I didn't really know what was going on. Then the doorbell rang.

My brothers jumped to their feet. Dad raced down the stairs. I just sat there in my sweatpants and T-shirt with syrup on my face and probably in my hair, too.

"I'll get it!" Dad practically shouted. He took a deep breath and smiled at all three of us, all but quivering with excitement. Dad had a reputation for being one of the most sophisticated, well-traveled men in East Shore, a reputation that would have been shot down pretty fast if people could only have seen him at home.

I took my own deep breath. Dad opened the door.

My *Sports Illustrated* man was tall. That was my first thought. My second thought followed quickly: *Wait until*

Ellie sees what I found! This man could make anyone forget about Josh Callahan. He had a movie star kind of glow.

He stuck out his hand.

"Tony DiMarco?" he asked as he shook hands with Dad. "It's a pleasure. I've been reading your column for years." He smiled, sort of. His teeth were perfect. "Ross-Berwick-*Sports-Illustrated,*" he said. He talked so fast I almost didn't understand him.

"Welcome to East Shore," Dad said. He smiled his professional smile, reputation intact.

"It's nice to be up here in this part of the world. Definitely off the beaten track," Mr. Berwick said. "What's it like working up here? You're so far away from everything that's really happening in sports."

Dad smiled again. "It's the road not taken. But it suits my style."

Mr. Berwick nodded. "You're the last of a breed."

"A dinosaur, you mean," Dad said.

"Oh, no, no!" Mr. Berwick said, laughing. "Thoughtful, passionate, articulate work will never be extinct. It just doesn't pay, that's all."

Dad laughed, too, and they shook hands again, as if some agreement had been reached.

Mr. Berwick strode over to Joe and Lou, shaking hands with both of them and showing them his teeth.

"Ross-Berwick-*Sports-Illustrated,*" he repeated. "It's a pleasure, boys."

Then he saw me, still sitting at the kitchen table.

Hi, Mr. Illustrated, I wanted to say, but I couldn't say something like that without Ellie at my side.

"You must be the mighty Ruth," he said. I nodded hesitantly, as if I wasn't quite sure.

He leaned over to me, his face just inches from mine. He reached out as if to shake my hand but then seemed to change his mind with his hand in midair. He sort of patted the top of my head instead, further messing up my hair.

"Hi, honey. I'm Ross," he said softly, and I didn't know whether I wanted to hug him or hit him.

I took my time getting dressed. Then I sat at the bottom of the stairs, out of view, listening to my father and brothers pepper Ross with questions while he ate French toast. My French toast. My *Sports Illustrated* interview. About me.

Finally Dad brought Ross over to me and escorted us to the front porch. He handed each of us a tall glass of orange juice and pointed to two lawn chairs.

"Ross says he'd like to get to know you," Dad explained. "I'll keep your brothers busy while you two talk."

I sat in my chair and stretched out my legs, brushing some imaginary dust off my jeans.

"You're tall for your age, aren't you?" Ross said.

I shrugged. "I guess. A little."

"Are you the tallest kid in your class?"

"No."

"Tallest girl?"

"No." I looked at him. "I mean, I'm not that tall. Just a little on the tall side."

"How tall was your mother?" Ross asked.

I stiffened. *Was.* I heard it. *Was.* He already knew. I wondered if he knew more.

"I don't know," I said, still looking at him. "How tall are you?"

He raised his eyebrows, surprised by my question. "Six four," he said.

"Did you ever play basketball?" I asked.

"Yes."

"Baseball?"

"Yes."

"Good," I said. "So are you staying for the district final on Friday? That's going to be the biggest game of the year so far."

"I know," Ross said. "I've done my research. And yes, I'm staying." He smiled a real smile. It was kind of nice. I decided to keep going.

"So, how old are you?"

"Thirty-seven."

"Married?"

"No." Ross took a long sip of orange juice. "Ruth," he said, "you can ask me anything you want. But I'm going to have to ask you some pretty personal questions, too. Okay?"

I didn't know if it was okay or not. I wasn't sure what a personal question from this man would be.

"I thought we were going to talk about baseball," I said.

"Baseball is only part of the story," Ross explained. "You are the more interesting part."

"I'm not that interesting," I said. "You know, without baseball, I'm . . ." I stopped suddenly as I heard in my mind what I was about to say.

Ross leaned forward. "What are you?" he asked. His voice was gentle. "Without baseball, what are you?"

I stared down the street. I could see the roof of Ellie's house behind a cluster of oak trees, and then beyond that, past my line of vision, were the beach and Ellie's dune.

"I'm nothing," I said softly. "Without baseball I am nothing special at all."

We were both silent. Ross finished his orange juice. He held the glass in his hands, rolling it back and forth between his palms.

"We need to play, you know," he said finally.

"We? Play?" I asked, not sure what he was getting at.

Ross smiled. "We. You and me. We need to mix it up a little, go one-on-one, pitcher to batter, batter to fielder, really go at it."

I shot up straight on the edge of my seat, practically sputtering, almost laughing. This was more like it. I was only too happy to get Ross out of my head and onto the field.

"No problem! You got it," I said. "Just name the time and place."

Ross actually laughed out loud, and his eyes were shining. It struck me that he looked pretty happy with himself for getting such a reaction out of me. I sat back slowly and folded my arms across my chest.

"We can play tomorrow afternoon, wherever you usually play, for as long as you want," he said. "And then, when you get tired and need a break, we can talk some more."

I took the bait, even though I knew he was teasing. "Well, don't count on talking tomorrow," I said, "because I can play all day."

"Then let me ask you another question right now, just in case," he said. "I don't know how much you've thought about this already, but . . . Where do you want to go with this game?"

My fingers curled around the armrests of my lawn chair. "What do you mean?" I asked, my voice fading away.

Ross shrugged as if he hadn't just asked the most important question in the world. "I mean," he said, "do you want to coach someday, or play in a women's league, maybe switch to softball, or maybe be a baseball writer, like your father? Something like that?"

I didn't say anything. I couldn't say anything. I felt as if I was sinking, in over my head, and the bottom of the ocean was still a long way off.

"Or maybe," Ross said slowly, as if the idea had just come to him, "maybe you want to be like your mother, only on a bigger stage."

I had totally lost control of the conversation, and I knew it. I could not think of anything safe or funny or creative to say, but I knew I had to say something.

"I've always wanted to play for the New York Yankees. Everybody knows that."

I wasn't smiling when I said it, and Ross did not smile when he heard it.

"You're eleven?" he asked, as if he didn't already know.

I nodded.

"And you still think about that, about playing for the Yankees?"

I looked straight at him. "Yes," I said.

"Well, good for you," Ross said, but I didn't believe him. He stood up and stretched. "I'm planning to go to your team practice this afternoon. I'd like to meet some of your teammates, get a feel for the community."

He stood right there on the porch, still holding his empty juice glass, ready to go back into the house and waiting for me to join him. I didn't move.

"Ruth?" he asked, looking in my direction, but I would not allow our eyes to meet. "Just one more question: Do you ever wish you were a boy?"

I tried not to flinch. I stared up at him blankly, but my mind was racing. I could think of lots of ways to answer that question that would tell him exactly nothing. What would Ellie say? Something funny and creative, for sure. What would Dad want me to say? I could only hope he wasn't hanging out in the house somewhere, listening. What would Mama have said?

"All the time," was what I finally chose to say, suddenly realizing that it was the truth.

Chapter 4

"**B**etter-looking than Josh Callahan? Are you serious?"

Ellie was talking a little too loudly, but no one was around so it was okay. She danced alongside me as we cut through a whole bunch of people's backyards on our way to Mitchell Community Park, home field of the East Shore All-Stars.

"Ellie, I'm talking about a *man,*" I said, hugging my glove tightly. "Josh Callahan is a child next to Ross. Not even in the same league."

Ellie bopped me on the head with her scorecard. She took notes for Coach Jameson at most of our games and practices. It was an Ellie kind of job, and she liked it. She could make anything interesting.

"You know something, Ruth?" she said, smiling. "I've never heard you talk this way about any guy. You must have one major crush on him."

"No way!" I shouted as Ellie burst out laughing. "I just met Ross this morning. I don't even really like him. He thinks he's got me all figured out or something. He's kind of a know-it-all jerk."

"But a good-looking know-it-all jerk," Ellie added, determined to get in the last word. "Anyway, I'm dying to meet him."

"You will," I said. "I think he wants to live my life all week. I know he's sticking around for Friday's game, and he's coming to practice this afternoon. He's probably already there."

We circled a thick patch of bushes in the corner of somebody's yard and stepped out onto Mitchell Road, across the street from the baseball field. My baseball field. I had played on it for my entire life, and I knew every corner, every slippery spot, every divot that could cause a bad hop. So much had happened on that baseball field; I had grown up on it. I wondered if all those years had been erased by my memories of last Saturday. I wondered if the field was as haunted as I was.

"Looks like everybody else is already there, too," Ellie said, interrupting my thoughts. "You must be fashionably late again."

Of course I was. I was always late for practice. I sort

of enjoyed showing up after everyone else was already on the field. I didn't know why, really. Maybe it was because I could.

We crossed the street. It did look as if the whole team was there, except me. Coach Jameson had already started the infield drills, and all the outfielders were crowded around Coach Dillon in center field. I wasn't wearing a watch, but it didn't take a genius to figure out that I was definitely later than usual, late even for me.

"Doesn't matter," I said to Ellie. "What're they going to do? Bench me?"

Ellie grabbed my arm. "Look! Over there." She pointed to a man sitting alone in the stands. "Is that him?"

It was. Ross was sitting in the middle of the grandstand with his feet resting on the seat in front of him and his elbows leaning back on the seat behind him. He looked about ready to doze off. But he still looked pretty cool, too.

"Ruth," Ellie said softly, "I mean . . . like . . . he's really *old*."

For some reason, I was totally insulted.

"I told you he was a grown man. And he's not that old. Who cares, anyway?" I glared at Ellie.

"Come on," she said, her voice getting louder. "He could be your father."

"He's a lot younger than my father!" I shouted.

Ross turned around, looking in our direction.

"Oh, great, now look what you've done," I whispered through clenched teeth.

"Me!" Ellie whispered back. "You're the one who started screaming."

"Shut up. He's staring at us." I waved at Ross. "Just act casual," I said to Ellie.

"We blew casual a long time ago," she said. "And I don't understand why this guy has you so worked up. I mean, I'll take Josh Callahan any day."

"You can have him," I said, looking toward the field. "I better get over there. Wait for me after practice, okay?"

"I always do," Ellie called after me in a singsong voice. She tried to give me a dirty look but fell far short of pulling it off. Ellie wouldn't stay mad long. She could not stop herself from being happy.

I stood on the sidelines near third base for several minutes. Coach Jameson acted as if he didn't even know me. He was at home plate, hitting high bouncing grounders to all the other infielders.

"Sorry I'm late, Coach," I said the first time he looked in my direction.

"Just stand there until I'm ready to deal with you, DiMarco," he said.

I glanced over at Ross to see if he was watching the mighty Ruth get disciplined. He waved at me. Wonderful. I waved back. This was just great material for a *Sports Illustrated* article. And there was Ellie, sitting about five rows behind Ross with her scorecard on her knees. She was checking him out for sure. I could only hope she was doing it quietly.

Coach Jameson made me sit out the whole infield drill. I watched Matt Paterson, my backup at shortstop, field my position pretty cleanly. Matt was a good, solid shortstop and a really nice guy. Sometimes I felt kind of bad that he never got a chance to play in a game that meant anything.

Cal Landry didn't seem to appreciate Matt's skills, though. Cal was our second baseman, my partner in the best double-play combination East Shore had ever seen. He kept looking over at me and pretending to gag himself with his index finger whenever Matt didn't make a play exactly the way I would have. Cal was obnoxious, but he was my best friend on the team.

"Everybody in!" Coach Jameson called out, signaling the end of the defensive drills and the beginning of batting practice. Coach Dillon took the mound, and Coach Jameson headed in my direction. He threw his arm around my shoulders and marched me to the left-field fence in foul territory.

Coach Jameson liked to think he was the fatherly type. Coach Dillon was still in college and looked even younger, but he couldn't quite pass for twelve, otherwise I swear he would've tried to suit up to play. Coach Dillon loved baseball almost as much as Dad or Joe or Lou. Or me.

Anyway, it was definitely Coach Jameson who handled all the disciplinary stuff.

"I don't like people being late to my practices, DiMarco," he said. He was talking right into my ear as if he thought I might have something wrong with my hearing.

"I know," I said.

"Even you," he said.

"I know."

"I can't afford to bench you on Friday."

"I know."

"The team wouldn't like it, the parents wouldn't like it, and your Mr. Berwick out there . . ." Coach nodded toward Ross. "He *really* wouldn't like it, now, would he?"

"No."

"Coming all the way to Maine just to watch you play baseball and then some local yokel fisherman coach benches you? No, your Mr. Berwick wouldn't like that at all."

Coach was on a roll. I didn't say anything. My head hurt. And Ross was staring at us from out in the stands, probably wishing he had a pair of binoculars so that he could read our lips.

"DiMarco?" Coach was still talking. "You okay?"

"I'm fine," I said softly. "I'm always fine."

"You know I need you to be on time, don't you?"

"I know."

"You know I still love you, don't you?"

I looked at Coach Jameson. My gruff and graying "fisherman coach" was at his fatherly best. He smiled. I couldn't help smiling a little, too.

"I know," I said. "But I don't love you back."

Coach shoved me gently toward home plate.

"Get out there and show your Mr. Berwick what you can do," he said. "And DiMarco?" He caught my arm. "Don't do this to me again. Got it?"

"Got it," I said. "And I'm really sorry," I added, because, after all, Coach had just said he loved me.

I crushed the ball.

My head was throbbing and I was having trouble keeping my mind on what I was doing, but my swing was just plain on. The ball looked like a balloon coming in to the plate in slow motion, and I couldn't stop myself from hammering it. Coach Dillon was practically laughing between pitches.

"Man!" he called from the mound. "What did Coach J. say to you? We got to use those magic words on everybody!"

I looked out to the grandstand to see if Ross was watching, but all I saw was Ellie standing out there alone, waving her arms at me. She was pointing in my direction or maybe behind me. I looked over my shoulder. Ross was hanging out by the backstop talking to Cal Landry and Sam Beals, who was our best pitcher and Cal's cousin. I needed to get over there fast. Cal had a big mouth, especially when he was with Sam, and he thought nothing of using it to say something embarrassing.

"I'm done," I said to Coach Dillion, holding up my hand. "I feel good."

"Your swing's looking great," he said. "I wish we could clone you."

I handed my bat to Matt Paterson. He stepped up to the plate and dug in.

"That bat's not going to help you, Paterson," Coach Dillon called out.

"I can hope, can't I?" Matt said. He smiled in my direction but didn't really look at me.

"Man, all you got is hope. Must be tough being the guy who sits out for Supergirl here." Coach Dillon was really having fun, but I wasn't sure at whose expense.

Matt played right along. "It's killing me, Coach," he said. "My self-esteem is shot."

"I bet it is," Coach said. "With your luck, you'll still be her backup when you both get drafted by the New York Yankees!"

Shut up, I wanted to say, but Matt and Coach Dillon laughed. Not so long before, I would have laughed, too. Not so long before, I wouldn't have known it was all such a big joke.

I turned to Ross, who smiled and nodded at me. He heard everything. I got the feeling he didn't miss much.

"What's up, guys?" I asked Cal and Sam.

"And the best thing about Ruth," Cal was saying loudly as he wrapped his arm around my neck in a make-believe headlock, "is that she doesn't do anything like a girl at all. I mean, she runs like a guy, throws like a guy, hits like a guy, and plays shortstop like a guy. You know, if I didn't have eyes, I'd swear she *was* a guy!"

Cal and Sam laughed as if they'd never heard anything so funny in their lives. Ross raised his eyebrows at me, looking as if he was trying pretty hard to keep a straight face himself.

Cal's headlock turned into a hug, sort of.

"But I'm real glad I got eyes," he said, and he and Sam laughed so loudly that they almost drowned out Ross.

Chapter 5

My bedroom was the smallest room in the house, but its one window faced west, allowing the sun to stream through the blinds late into the evening, almost until bedtime. I loved my room. It was where I went when I absolutely needed to be alone. Being alone was important to me sometimes. Joe said I needed my space in a house full of men. Lou said I needed to sulk. And I said I needed to think deep thoughts. I wasn't sure who was right.

But I knew I wanted to be alone right after baseball practice, right through listening to Ross and the guys laughing their faces off, right through walking home with Ellie, right through eating supper with Dad and my brothers. As soon as I cleared the table, I announced I was going to bed and practically ran upstairs. I sat on my bed feeling miserable, and then my vision blurred and my nose began to run and I felt even worse. And then, as if I really needed it, Dad knocked on my door.

"I'm coming in," he announced, not exactly asking a question but still waiting for a response.

"Why?" I asked. "Nothing exciting going on in here. I'm just getting ready for bed."

"Something's bothering you, and I'm coming in," Dad said.

I stared at the door. It stayed shut. I didn't know what Dad was afraid of, but ever since I'd started middle school he'd seemed incapable of opening my bedroom door.

"Dad, I'm completely dressed, you know," I said, and then the door did actually open, slowly.

Dad didn't come into my room very often, and he looked strange in it, too big and awkward. He sat next to me on the bed and managed to seem a little more in proportion.

"I'm okay, Dad," I said before he could say anything. "Just tired after practice, that's all."

Dad looked into my blurry eyes, and I knew he didn't believe me.

"Tell me the truth, now, Babe," he said. "Is it too much pressure? The all-star team and Ross being here and the article and all?"

"No, that's not it." I took a quick look at Dad's face, all concerned and everything. I chose my words carefully, for maximum effect. "I don't know," I said. "Maybe I'm just outgrowing baseball. Maybe I don't like it so much anymore."

There. I'd said it. It wasn't true, but I'd said it anyway—the most shocking words anyone named DiMarco could ever say. I waited for Dad to fall to pieces.

But he stayed calm. He reached out and hugged me close. He almost seemed . . . happy.

"It's okay, Babe," he said. "You don't have to play baseball anymore. You don't even have to *like* baseball anymore." He smiled and brushed my hair away from my face with his hand. "You're becoming a young woman, you know," he continued. "You're going to be interested in a lot of things, and it's okay if baseball isn't one of them."

I wanted to scream. It shouldn't have been that easy. I was tired of easy. Dad was trying to be all nice and sensitive, and I hated it. He'd gotten it all wrong. I wanted him to yell at me, to tell me that I had to play baseball, that it was a family tradition and I was part of it. I wanted him to scream at the top of his lungs that I was just too good to quit.

But Dad didn't yell at all. Neither did I. I stared out the window and tried to imagine what would happen if I suddenly had a total temper tantrum. I would throw myself on the floor and kick my feet and scream about how no one understood me and no one cared and how the only thing that mattered to me in my whole entire life was baseball and now everyone was trying to ruin that, too. I would scream and scream and scream and everything I screamed would be the absolute truth and I would scream all those things that I could never say in a normal voice.

I want to play in the major leagues.

I want you to believe in me.

I want Mama!

And then I thought about how Dad would react. He would die. He would look at me as if I was a total stranger and probably pass right out. Or maybe he would scream back. Maybe he would scream something like he never wanted a daughter in the first place, that I was just complicating his life, and if I wasn't happy I might as well leave. Maybe. Actually, I had no idea how Dad would react. And not knowing scared me more than anything I could possibly imagine.

So I didn't say anything. Or at least not much. I looked up at Dad, who was still holding me close. He had such a nice look on his face, as if he didn't want to be anyplace else in the world. I knew he loved me. But that wasn't enough.

"Don't worry about me, Dad," I said. "I'm okay with baseball and everything. It's just that maybe it's not baseball I'm outgrowing, maybe it's the team or something."

"Could be," Dad said, smiling. "Girls your age do mature faster than boys."

I stared out the window again, dreaming and talking mostly to myself. "Wouldn't it be great to skip all this and play with people who are older and better? You know, like major leaguers?"

Dad laughed out loud. "You're funny, Babe," he said. "One minute you're talking about outgrowing the whole sport and the next minute you're talking about playing in the major leagues." He shook his head. "Glad to hear you're not too old for dreams."

I stood up. My legs were shaking. Dreams. Dad said it, and I understood: In Dad's mind, it was all but over. My baseball life was coming to a close. And it was time for me to wake up.

"I'm tired," I said. "I think I'm going to get ready for bed."

"Good night, Baby Ruth." Dad kissed my forehead. "Sweet dreams. Hit a grand slam in the majors for me."

I waited until Dad had left the room. As soon as he'd shut the door behind him, I threw myself on the floor and kicked my feet wildly, being careful not to hit anything. I didn't dare make any noise. No one could ever know that I was rolling around on my bedroom floor having a full-blown temper tantrum, lost in a wild dreamworld that I had always thought was reality.

"Don't mind me," I said to the ceiling. "I'm just busy becoming a young woman. Dad said so."

I thought it might be a good time to cry, but I couldn't seem to remember how.

I fell asleep on the floor. I must have, because the next thing I knew, I was crawling on my hands and knees, guided by the dull glow of the moonlight that filled my room. I reached under the bed for my scrapbooks.

I found Mama's first. I opened it slowly, as if I didn't quite know what to expect, but there they were, the same as always, all the articles and photographs I knew so well: Mama running through the obstacle course during the firefighter physical fitness test, Mama getting the highest score on the written exam, Mama in formal uniform for the first time, and that wonderful photograph of Mama, smiling and proud in her brand-new firefighter gear, holding the hand of a little girl, still almost a baby, who looks as if she knows there isn't anyone in the world as wonderful as her mother.

And then came the obituary. And the eulogies. And all the sad and wonderful letters to the editor proclaiming Mama a hero, a woman with a vision, a woman in whom all of East Shore took great pride. Such a shame she had to die so young. And the rest of the pages in the scrapbook were blank.

I pulled out my scrapbook next and saw pictures of me, me in uniform, too, different uniforms, rising through the ranks of the East Shore Little League. Then there were columns and lists of standings and statistics, batting average, home runs, RBIs, fielding percentage, and the name Ruth DiMarco, always, always on top.

And there were articles, so many articles, with headlines like SOMETHING SPECIAL and PHENOM! and THE PRIDE OF EAST SHORE, and a long editorial, four columns wide, titled THIS GIRL CAN PLAY.

I flipped to the end of the scrapbook, where the pages were blank, waiting to be filled, or maybe blank like Mama's, blank forever, because the entire story had already been told.

Saturday afternoon
***—bottom of the 3rd, bases empty, no outs, Red Hill
1, East Shore 4***

*I don't know what to expect as I step up to the plate
and I don't really care. I do know that I probably won't
be seeing any more big fat fastballs right down the middle. The pitcher tried to blow one by me in the first inning, and I took it deep over the center-field fence. I
didn't have to think for that one; it was automatic. My
father once said that I can pick up a fastball earlier than
Ted Williams. I believed him.*

*I barely notice that the catcher is talking to me until
he repeats himself, his voice a little louder.*

*"You going to hit the next one out of here, too?" he
asks.*

"Uh-huh," I say. "You got it."

"I bet you can hit one out anytime you feel like it," he

says, and his voice is weird, not mean but taunting, and I don't know why.

"That's right," I say, nodding but not looking at him. I know who he is. His name is Sean, I think, and he's the kind of guy who will intentionally bump into you at the mall or somewhere so he can say he's sorry while running his hand up your back to check if you've got a bra on.

I wonder what he's thinking about right now.

"I think everybody will just about go crazy if you hit this one out even deeper than the last one," he says.

"Uh-huh," I say, and I watch the pitcher go into his windup. He's throwing junk now, off-speed stuff, going for the outside corner of the plate but missing. He tries the same pitch again and this time gets the call.

"Not giving you much to hit," Sean says. "I think he's afraid of you."

"Probably," I say.

"Still think you're gonna hit one out?"

"Uh-huh."

Then the same pitch is coming in to the exact same spot, and I reach across the plate with my bat straight out and flick a short, dead bunt up the third-base line. I fly toward first base, listening to Sean swear as he tears off his mask and chases the ball. I'm standing on first before he can even get off a throw.

I smile. He spits in my direction.

Nothing much happens the rest of the inning, and I'm

left stranded on first. I make a point of walking past Sean as I head to the dugout, and he seems only too happy to see me.

"Nice bunt," he says.

"Thank you," I say.

"I don't know," he says, "there's just something I can't get out of my head."

He's got that weird voice going again. I look at him. He smiles.

"I don't know," he says again, "but by the time we're all in high school, do you think anyone will even remember your name?"

Chapter 6

I woke up in my bed the next morning, a little confused about how I got there and kind of embarrassed when I remembered rolling around on the floor. I dressed quickly and quietly and grabbed my glove, planning to sneak out of the house before breakfast. I did not need to see Dad or Joe or Lou first thing in the morning. I needed Ellie.

I needed Ellie to talk me into helping her with one of her projects, like building a life-size sand castle or trailing twenty feet behind Josh Callahan for a whole day. I needed Ellie and her big old sprawling eleven-room house with three libraries and two studies and books absolutely everywhere. I needed Ellie to make me laugh, and I needed Ellie to listen to me talk about Mama.

Ellie's mother was wearing her green plaid flannel bathrobe, searching for something on the front porch, when I showed up. She smiled when she saw me and stood up tall with her hands on her hips. She had shoulder-length, curly reddish brown hair, too; it was just like Ellie's but without the wildness.

"Good morning, Ms. DiMarco," she greeted me. "Did your family receive a newspaper this morning, by any chance?"

I nodded. "It was right on the front steps, Ms. Quinn," I said. Ellie's mother had seen no reason to change her last name when she married Ellie's father. I thought that was about the coolest thing in the world to do. Or not to do. I wondered why Mama had not.

"Sometimes Mr. Callahan's aim is quite poor, I'm afraid," Ms. Quinn said.

I pictured Josh whipping by Ellie's house on his bike, wildly throwing the paper toward the porch, scared to death someone was watching him and knowing for sure that someone always was.

"Ma!" Ellie called from inside the house. "I already picked up the paper this morning. It was right at the door."

Ellie's mother cupped her hand around her mouth as if she was telling a secret. "My guess is that Ms. Sanders was waiting for Mr. Callahan's arrival quite early this morning," she whispered loudly.

"My guess is that you're right," I whispered back.

Ms. Quinn's laugh sounded like singing. She held out her hand for me to take. "Would you like to come in for breakfast, then, love?" she asked. "I'd say you could use a break from all that testosterone at your house."

"You're right about that, too," I said, taking her hand. Ellie's mother had come to Maine from Ireland when she was eighteen. I loved her brogue and the way she could make me laugh. Her hand was soft and smooth. My hands were hardened by calluses from years of gripping a baseball bat and making bare-handed plays at shortstop. I decided to buy a bottle of hand lotion to use every morning for the rest of my life.

Ms. Quinn led me to the kitchen, to Ellie, who was sitting at the table slicing strawberries to add to a big bowl of pancake batter.

"They're great," Ellie said, popping a strawberry into her mouth. "My dad picked them yesterday. First of the season. Are you staying for breakfast?" She pushed the bowl of strawberries across the table toward me. I sat next to Ellie, placed my glove on the table, and took a strawberry, holding it gently in the palm of my hand.

"Ellie," I said softly. "Ellie, my mother was a feminist."

Ellie nodded and turned her eyes away from me as if the strawberries now needed her full attention. Her mother placed her hand on top of my head lightly and then picked up the bowl of pancake batter.

"I'll start the pancakes while the two of you talk," she said.

"That's okay, Ma." Ellie jumped to her feet. "I'll do it."

"No, no," her mother said, gently pushing Ellie back into her seat. "I will."

Ellie's cheeks were pink, but I didn't care.

"I was up late last night reading the articles in my mother's scrapbook," I told Ellie because I needed her to know. "She was a real feminist—she really believed that she could do whatever she wanted to. In one of the articles it said that she dreamed about being a firefighter all her life, even when she was younger than we are."

"You're a feminist, too, Ruth," Ellie said, her voice low. "You're a bigger feminist than I am. You're living it."

"But I've never even really thought about it!" I exclaimed. "Not like my mother. Not like you. All I've ever thought about is being a baseball player."

I stopped because I could hear my voice rising. I didn't know what I was going to say next.

"It's nice then, that your mother was able to see her dream come true . . . sort of," Ellie said, her voice fading away, unsure.

"Do you think so?" I asked, wanting Ellie to say more. "Do you really think she felt that way? Like her dreams were coming true?"

"Sure, Ruth . . . I—I don't know," Ellie stammered. "Sure . . . I guess so."

"I wonder if she was proud, proud of her life," I said, "or if she wanted more. What do you think, El?"

"Oh, Ruth," Ellie practically whispered. "You know I can't talk to you about your mother."

I did not want to hear what Ellie was trying to tell me. "Why not?" I asked. "We never talk about her. What's wrong with talking about my mother?"

"She's not here!" Ellie burst out, her voice cracking, and only then did I see the tears welling up in her eyes.

But my mind was clouded. I could not think about what Ellie was saying. I only knew I wasn't finished.

"Of course she's not here," I said, vaguely aware of the harshness of my words. "She's never been here. She's been dead for practically my whole life."

Ellie fidgeted in her seat. "I don't know what to say, Ruth," she said. "It's horrible, I know. I can't even imagine it."

"You don't need to imagine it," I said. "I'm right here."

Ellie didn't say anything. I waited, waited for something to happen, something to get the conversation back on track. Finally Ellie's mother appeared next to us and gently placed a plate of pancakes on the table.

"You can share these," she said. "I'll be out back in the garden. Call me if you need me for anything." She practically glided out of the kitchen. Ellie looked as if she wanted to tackle her.

I started to reach for a fork but stopped when I caught sight of my hand. Seedy red pulp oozed from between the fingers of my still-clenched fist. Ellie handed me a napkin. That was all the contact I needed.

"Ross asked if I wanted to be like my mother, only on a bigger stage," I said. "What do you think that's supposed to mean?"

"I don't know," Ellie said, but then she continued: "Maybe he meant that playing baseball is going to get you a lot more attention than putting out fires ever got your mother. I mean, it's not like there's a magazine out there called *Firefighters Illustrated*."

I stared at her. I didn't know why I suddenly had to struggle to keep a straight face.

"Oh my God," Ellie said, her words rising to a squeak. "Did I really just say that? That is so dumb!"

"Highly dumb," I said, trying to stay serious, but I knew I was about to start squeaking myself.

"What are *you* laughing at?" Ellie gasped, a smile bursting across her face. "This is so not funny."

"It's hysterical. The whole thing is hysterical." I buried my face in my hands. My shoulders shook. "I am not laughing," I said, gasping. "I refuse to laugh."

Ellie put her head down on the table and breathed deeply. "What is our problem?" she asked after a moment.

"You mean, why can't we talk about my mother?" I said. I peeked out at her from between my fingers.

Ellie nodded, her head still on the table.

"Let's get out of here," I said. I took my own deep breath and let my hands fall from my face. "Come with me to Mitchell Park. Ross wants me to meet him there to play catch or something."

Ellie sat up straight. She snatched up my glove and shoved it at me.

"I'll be the perfect third wheel," she said.

"The best," I said.

Chapter 7

"I could be better, you know," Ellie said as we crossed Mitchell Road.

I shielded my eyes from the sun with my glove and scanned the field. There was no sign of Ross yet. I hoped he would show up soon. Nothing would feel better than a hard game of catch or making solid contact on a fastball thrown by an adult. I wanted to play.

We climbed the infield fence, and Ellie hit the ground running. She scooted over to the pitcher's mound and sat down, patting the space beside her. I squatted next to her and studied the distance from the mound to home plate. I wondered how I looked to the Red Hill pitcher when he went into his windup. The mighty Ruth.

"I could be better," Ellie said again.

I looked over my shoulder, across the field, toward the parking lot. No Ross.

"Better at what?" I asked.

"I could be a better best friend."

"Oh, Ellie," I said, still not looking at her. "So what? So could I."

"It's your one flaw, you know, not having a mother. Otherwise you'd be too perfect." Ellie was speaking quickly, almost rushing her words. She took a deep breath, slowing down. "But it's an awfully big flaw. I do know that, Ruth."

So we were still trying to talk about Mama, sort of.

"Well, you're pretty perfect yourself," I said.

"No." Ellie shook her head. "If I'm perfect at anything it's all the wrong things. That's why there's no Little League for readers or actors or artists. Or feminists."

I looked at Ellie. "I hear you," I said. "I'm definitely perfect at the right thing, but I'm the wrong person to be perfect at it."

"But still, Ruth," Ellie said, "you come out okay. I mean, all the boys at school like you because it would be really uncool not to. And all the girls like you because they're all hoping that maybe the boys will like them, too. By association or something."

"I'm okay *now*, Ellie," I said softly, but I knew she wasn't really hearing me. She had too much to say.

"You know," she continued, "the fact that you are my best friend saves me at school. It's the most perfect thing about me."

I looked away again, back at the parking lot, at the sky, anywhere.

"Come on, Ruth," Ellie said. "It's true, isn't it? You know it's true."

"Yes!" I said forcefully, as I suddenly realized that I really did agree. I turned to Ellie. "It *is* true, but . . . it shouldn't be."

Ellie looked a bit stunned for a moment, but then her face relaxed into a smile.

"Weird Friend Illustrated," she said. "You think it's got a chance?"

"I'd read it," I said. "But I might be the only one."

"Look!" Ellie said suddenly. "There he is." She hopped to her feet and pointed across the field toward the parking lot. I straightened up slowly and stretched, trying to act relaxed as every drop of blood in my body rushed to my face.

Ross cut across the parking lot and walked through the gate to the outfield. He had a bag of bats slung over his right shoulder, and he was carrying a bag of baseballs and a glove in his left hand. I recognized the bags immediately: They both belonged to Coach Jameson. I figured out then that Coach J. had to know about Ross meeting me at the field, and that meant that they had been talking, talking all about me. I wondered if Ross needed Coach's permission to play with me, or if he even had to ask Dad.

"So you brought your buddy along," Ross said as he crossed second base.

Ellie smiled brightly. "I'm the chaperone," she announced.

"Oh my God, Ellie," I whispered, turning my back to Ross. "Please shut up."

"That's okay," Ross said. He dropped the bat bag and the baseball bag in the middle of the infield, between second base and the pitcher's mound. "She can watch."

"I can shag, too," Ellie added. "Like when Ruth hits everything past you and you get tired of running around."

"That'd be fine, thank you," Ross said, grinning. He slipped his glove onto his left hand and picked a ball out of the bag. "Come on out to the outfield," he said to me. "Let's get moving." He jogged to left center field, and I headed to right center.

We started off slowly, lobbing the ball to each other, loosening up our throwing arms. Then Ross started to put more heat on the ball, throwing harder and harder as he also took steps backward, lengthening the distance between us. This was a test, after all.

I quickly realized two things. First, Ross could throw hard, definitely harder than any of my teammates, probably harder than Dad, too, but not quite as hard as Joe. And second, I realized that I could keep up with him. His ball popped loudly into my glove, and I loved the sharp, snapping sound. I reached out and grabbed the ball as it was coming at me, faster and faster, letting the webbing of my glove snatch the ball out of the air, protecting my hand from absorbing the sting. It was beautiful.

And then, gradually, I began to throw harder, too, really opening up my shoulder and letting my arm snap through the motion. Dad taught all of us very early on that throwing hard had less to do with strength than with having a loose, "live" arm. Dad also said that I was probably particularly loose-jointed; I could always fling my arm through the air easily and naturally and throw the ball in a hard, straight line.

Ross held up his glove first.

"Hey," he called. "I've had enough." He jogged toward me smoothly. He had a nice long stride. He stopped in front of me and looked at me closely, as if he might be seeing me for the first time.

"You okay?" I asked, trying to tease him.

He smiled. "I'm fine," he said. "It's just that I want to be able to lift up my arm tomorrow." He paused for a moment and looked over at Ellie, who was lying on her back in the sun over in foul territory. Then he turned to me again. "Great arm," he said softly. "Smart glove, too. I'd like to see you at shortstop now. Mind if I hit you a few?"

"No problem," I said. "You don't want me to make a throw?"

"Just toss the ball over the foul line," he answered. "I don't think our Ellie is quite up to playing first base."

Ross smiled as I laughed. I had to give him credit. Lots of people couldn't seem to figure out Ellie at all, but Ross was definitely right on track.

Something happened to Ross while we were playing. It was nothing he said or did, just something I could sense.

He smacked hard, sharp ground balls to me, over and over, left and right, deep and shallow, testing my range at shortstop. I was running and leaping and diving all over the place, getting hot and sweaty and dirty, and I was loving it. I knew I could make the play.

Then, without saying much of anything, Ross decided it was time for batting practice. Ellie helped pick up the baseballs, and Ross strode to the mound with the full bag of balls and pointed to the plate. He pitched rapidly, emptying the bag quickly, barely pausing between pitches except for barking the occasional command: "Pull it! Opposite field! Take it deep! Up the middle!" And I responded: *Crack! Crack! Crack! Crack!*

This is me, I wanted to say to Ross. *This is where I am perfect.*

Finally Ross glanced at his watch, dropped his glove, and waved me in to the mound. He stood there with his hands on his hips and waited for Ellie to join us. Ellie glided up to me and threw an arm around my shoulders.

"So," she said to Ross, "what do you think of my girl?"

Ross stared at me. He shook his head and looked away for a moment; then he stared at me again.

"This is history," he said.

Ellie laughed.

I just stood there, right in the middle but really on the sidelines, waiting for one of them to say more.

"I mean," Ross continued, "this is rewriting history. This is Jackie Robinson. Only, you know, this is bigger than Jackie Robinson because everybody always knew that the guys in the Negro Leagues were as good as the guys in the major leagues, but nobody has ever, *ever* believed that a woman could be this good."

Ross dropped his hands from his hips, took a few steps off the mound, turned around, stepped back up on the mound, and brought his hands back up to his hips again. He was practically quivering.

"How good?" I asked.

"As good as you," he answered. "As good as anybody."

"I think," Ellie said dryly, "that you impressed him."

A car horn blared loudly, too close to be on the street, and all three of us turned to face the parking lot.

"Oh, look who's here. It figures," I said as we watched my brothers climb out of Joe's old Jeep. "They have their gloves with them, too. I didn't even tell them we were going to be here."

"But I did," Ross said simply. "Tell me, Ruth, can you hit your brother? I hear his fastball's been clocked at almost ninety miles an hour. That's pretty good for a high school pitcher."

"Joe? Well, sure," I answered. "I mean, Joe's a really good pitcher, but, yeah. I can hit him."

"Hey, guys," Ellie called out to my brothers as they jogged up to the infield.

"Okay, Joe," Ross said, all business. "Let's cut right to the chase. I want to see her hit you. I can't believe what I've seen so far. Are you warmed up? I want to see nothing but heat."

Joe smiled. "Unbelievable, isn't she?" He swatted the back of my head.

"You three get to work," Ross said to me and my brothers. "I need to see more *now*." He grabbed Ellie's hand. "Come on, little buddy," he said as he led her off the mound. "You and I need to get out of the line of fire."

Ellie turned and raised her eyebrows at me as she marched away with Ross. Joe took the mound, and Lou and I headed to home plate.

"Hey, Lou!" Ross called out suddenly. "Don't you have a mask?"

Lou waved off Ross with his catcher's mitt. "Don't worry about it," he said. "How many pitches do you think are actually going to reach me?"

Joe had already warmed up, but I let him throw a few before I stepped into the batter's box. He was throwing from several feet behind the pitcher's mound, closer to where a major-league mound would be. I watched Ross watch Joe. He nodded with each pitch. I could tell he was impressed with Joe's velocity.

For ten minutes, Joe pitched, I hit, and Lou crouched behind home plate.

I hit Joe the way I always did, spraying line drives to all fields. My brother threw hard, for sure, but it was easy for me to make good contact and hit the ball sharply. It was a little tougher for me to hit the ball deep, though, and when I tried too hard, that was when I would swing and miss. I wondered if Ross noticed, and what he would think. I hit only two out of the park.

"She owns you," Ross said to Joe as my brothers and I flopped down on the grass in foul territory, next to Ellie.

"Uh-huh. She always has," Joe said softly. He smiled. "And she hasn't even had a real growth spurt yet or started to lift weights or anything. She's all talent. She's got it all."

Lou snorted. Everybody turned to look at him. He seemed self-conscious for a moment but then shrugged.

"Joe's right, of course, but it seems so arbitrary, doesn't it?" he said. "I mean, Ruthie's got it all, and Joe and I have some of it. It's great for Ruthie and everything, but we're the ones who could use more. If we had what she's got, we could really go places—the sky would be the limit. I'm talking all the way to the majors."

I felt myself go cold. *What a shame*. I looked at Ross. He was staring at Lou.

Ellie took over.

"Do you even hear yourself?" she asked. She glared at Lou. My best friend, to the rescue.

"I'm not saying anything that's not true," Lou said evenly.

"The sky's the limit for Ruth, too," Ellie continued. "Why shouldn't it be? She's Jackie Robinson, right, Ross?"

"And she's Ruth DiMarco, too," Ross said. He smiled at Ellie. "But let me ask you kids a question. As Ruth gets older and becomes the darling of the media, including my magazine, how do you think East Shore will respond? This is a pretty small town."

I sat up straight. "You mean, because I'm a girl?" I asked. "I don't see why East Shore should be any different from any other place. I mean, this town did just fine with Mama." I turned to Ross. "You should see the pictures and articles in my scrapbook," I explained. "Mama was like a hero here. This town loved her—"

"Oh, shut up, Ruthie!" Lou shouted. He leaped to his feet. "Just shut up. You don't know what you're talking about."

My mouth hung open. Even Ellie was speechless.

"Easy, Lou." Ross's voice was soft but guarded. "If you've got something to say, why don't you tell us?"

"This. Pretty. Little. Town," Lou said, his words laced

with anger, "didn't know what to do with Mama. Dad's been protecting you for too long, Ruthie. He never showed you all those other articles, the ones that blasted Mama and him and all of us. And maybe they were right, you know? Mama did just what she wanted and got herself killed like she didn't care about any of us. What's so heroic about that?"

I didn't even see Joe get up, but the next thing I knew Lou was on the ground and Joe was standing over him and Ross was grabbing Joe. But I didn't care about any of that.

"Nothing he said was true, right, Joe?" I asked. "None of it?"

Joe didn't say anything. He looked over my head, past me, at nothing.

Lou rolled over and picked himself up off the ground.

"It's all true, Ruthie," he said. "And you know it. At least, it's about time you knew it."

Joe lunged at Lou again, but Ross pulled him back as Lou darted out of the way.

"Just get out of here!" Joe shouted at Lou, spraying saliva everywhere.

"I'm gone," Lou said. He snatched up his glove, vaulted over the infield fence, and disappeared through the parking lot.

I was still sitting in the grass. Ellie was right next to me, up close, watching me out of the corner of her eye.

"Everybody okay?" Ross asked softly. He was still holding Joe, but in a way that looked more as if he was holding my brother up than restraining him.

Joe was silent. He was still staring at nothing.

I had never seen my brothers so angry in my life.

I had never been so angry in my life.

I stood up slowly. "I have to go," I said, my voice flat. I started walking.

"Are you sure? Where?" Ross asked.

I kept walking until I reached the fence. I stuck my feet in the lower links and pulled myself to the top. I did not turn around, but I knew I had to say something, and I wanted it to be the truth.

"I'm going home to scream at my father," I finally said.

Chapter 8

"**S**ometimes I think I hate you," I said, but I wasn't screaming.

Dad was sitting at the dining room table with his back to me, hard at work on some new article, typing away as if everything was just fine with the world. He turned around and looked at me as if he was trying to figure out exactly where my voice was coming from.

"I thought you were out," he said. "Aren't you supposed to be playing ball with Ross and your brothers?"

"Did you hear me?" I asked, staring. "Sometimes I think I hate you."

Something flickered in Dad's face, and he stared right back at me.

"Well, this is just what I need," he said. "Mind telling me why?"

My hands and nose were freezing, and my legs began to quiver. I knew I had to sit down fast.

"You should already know why," I said, suddenly scared to death that I wasn't going to be able to tell him anything at all. There was nothing simple or easy about any of this. I slid into the chair across from him. Talk to him, I told myself, he's your father. *Tell Daddy.*

"Dad!" I cried, my voice louder than I wanted it to be. "I don't know anything about Mama. All I've got is a scrapbook that's all nicey-nicey and everything and doesn't even tell the whole truth. You never tell me anything. I have to get the truth from other people."

Dad's eyes were wide, but his voice was calm. "So, what do you want to know?"

"Mama blew it, didn't she?" I said, talking as fast as I could. "She just had to go out and be a firefighter and get herself killed and leave us all alone. Who did she think she was? Mama blew it."

Dad shoved himself away from the table. His chair crashed and skidded across the living room floor.

"Don't you dare talk about your mother like that!" he cried, his voice unlike anything I had ever heard before, gasping, suffocating.

"Why not?" I shouted back, stunned by the force behind my words. "At least I'm talking about her. You

68

never talk about her at all. And you should hear Lou. Why don't you ask him about Mama sometime?"

Dad looked right through me, his eyes not meeting mine. He looked right through me as if I wasn't even there.

"This conversation is over," he said, his voice steady, even, ice. He picked up his chair, placed it at the table again, and sat right back down, right back in control.

I wanted to throw myself at him. I wanted to leap into his lap and curl up in a little ball and feel his arms around me, forever.

"D-Dad?" I choked out, but I could not continue.

He stood up again, and for one terrible moment I thought he might leave the room, leave me sitting there alone. Then he came over to my side of the table and crouched down next to me.

"What do you want me to tell you?" he asked. "That your mother shouldn't have died? Well, she shouldn't have died, then. Nobody should ever die at her age when they still have so much life ahead of them."

Dad's face was inches away from mine, but he wasn't looking at me. He was staring off into space, not angry, not sad, not anything.

Good job, I said to myself, now look what you've done. My two brothers were screaming and fighting, and my father had become nothing.

"Dad?" I asked softly. "Could I maybe just see all the

articles you didn't put in Mama's scrapbook? You must still have them somewhere. Lou already told me about them, anyway."

Dad got up immediately and left the room. He was back in seconds, carrying a file folder. He placed the folder in my lap.

"They're yours, now," he said. "I thought you were too young, but . . . I don't know, maybe I made a mistake." He sighed like somebody who was determined not to cry.

"Can I take this upstairs?" I asked, holding up the folder.

Dad nodded, and I took off, running up the stairs two at a time, faster than usual. I realized with a rush of horror and satisfaction that I had never felt so powerful in my life.

There were only a handful of articles—five, to be exact—and they all said pretty much the same thing. I spread them out on my bed and sat in the middle. I turned to my right: AT WHAT COST EQUALITY? the headline blared. To my left: FIRE DEPARTMENT RE-EXAMINES QUEST FOR 'PROGRESS.' In front of me: A DANGEROUS JOB. Behind me: AND WHAT ABOUT THE CHILDREN?

The articles didn't attack Mama personally, but all of them questioned her desire to become a firefighter as well as the fire department's decision to hire her or any mother of three young children. Four of the articles were written by men. I was most interested in the fifth one, and I held it in my lap, saving it for last.

" 'A Woman's Choice,' by Judy McGowan," I read out loud. *Every woman has the right to choose a profession*, Ms. McGowan wrote. *But sometimes we make bad choices*.

I shivered with anger and a sense of loyalty I hadn't known I possessed. I might have expected it of the men, but how dare this woman criticize Mama? Mama would never have put herself at risk if it wasn't important. She was trying to rescue people from a fire. What was wrong with that? None of the writers would ever have said anything against Mama if they had really known her.

I shivered again as I suddenly remembered that I had never really known Mama, either.

I turned to the end of Ms. McGowan's article, and it was there that I saw the photograph, the same photograph, the one with Mama in full firefighter gear holding my hand when I was three years old, the one I had always thought was so wonderful.

I stared at my smiling, little-girl face, the face of a stranger, happy forever.

But I knew that nothing was forever. What happened after that picture was taken? What did the next picture of that little girl look like? What did she look like when they told her that her mother was dead?

I thought I knew, but I was afraid to look in the mirror.

Saturday afternoon
   —top of the 4th, runner on third, one out, Red Hill 1, East Shore 4

The ball is bouncing slowly up the middle and I know it's the shortstop's play, my play, and I know that if I charge the ball hard I might even have a chance at holding the runner on third and that, in any event, the out at first should be automatic. I know.

I also know that if I hang back and watch this play happen around me, Cal Landry will back me up perfectly, scooping up the ball and tossing the batter out at first, although he won't be able to do anything about stopping the guy on third from scoring. There won't be enough time.

So I don't move and watch Cal spring into action. He's good at what he does. In seconds there are two outs and one run in. The crowd gives Cal a nice hand for a *nice play. No one even seems to notice that it was my play and I did nothing at all. Almost no one. Coach Jameson stares at me, spreading his hands out wide and then tapping the side of his head. He thinks I wasn't thinking, that maybe I didn't recognize the play.*

I look into the stands behind the dugout. It strikes me how many people hold real conversations at baseball games, like they're not paying attention to the action, like they're not able to recognize all the really important little things that are happening on the field.

I look at Ellie and her mother. Their lips are moving fast and their hands are flying and I know they probably haven't shut up since the first pitch, but that's okay. I know Ellie and her mother always have a lot to talk about, and it's usually pretty interesting and never about baseball. They tell each other everything.

Two rows in front of them, I see Dad and Joe. Joe is gesturing with his hands as if he's holding a baseball bat and it doesn't take much to figure out that they're talking about baseball, all right, but I'm not at all sure they're talking about the baseball game right in front of them.

Then I see Lou and Josh Callahan sitting a few feet away from Dad and Joe, up the first-base line. They are not talking, and I can tell Lou is trying to catch my eye, but I won't quite look at him long enough for him to know I really see him. He's shaking his head at me like he's disappointed or disgusted or like he knows too much.

I turn away and pound my glove, watching the next batter dig into the batter's box. I feel myself get hot, hot and embarrassed, because I know what just happened, and I think Lou might know, too, and part of me wants to disappear while another part of me really, really wants to laugh out loud.

I wonder if Babe Ruth ever felt like this.

Chapter 9

I woke up mad Wednesday morning.

It felt good.

When the phone rang, I knew it was Ellie.

"I won't be at baseball practice today," she said. "Coach Jameson says he doesn't need me, and my father wants me to go to the lumberyard with him, anyway. He's building a shed in the backyard. Another one. My mother says if he builds one more we can all move out of the house and into our own individual sheds."

"Mmm," I murmured into the phone. "That's okay. Whatever."

"Are you all right, Ruth?" Ellie asked. Her voice was quiet, serious quiet, and I didn't want to deal with it.

"Uh-huh," I said. "There's no practice tomorrow. Maybe we can go to the beach."

"Sounds good," Ellie said just before hanging up. She sounded relieved. Ellie hated when things got awkward between people, especially if she wasn't the cause. She liked to feel she was a step ahead of everyone. But most of all, I knew Ellie wanted me to be happy. Like her.

I walked to practice alone, which was just fine with me. I needed to do some pretty serious thinking, and I did not need Ellie talking me out of anything. I wanted to stay mad, and I had made up my mind. I was going to tank Friday's district final against the Sacksport All-Stars, and I thought I might tank every game I played for the rest of my life until Babe Ruth himself sent me a message from heaven telling me to quit playing baseball for the good of the sport.

Quit playing baseball. Maybe that was what Dad really wanted. Maybe he wanted me to quit playing baseball before anybody could learn how my story might turn out. Maybe Dad would rather I quit than fail. Maybe that was what he wished Mama had done. Maybe he wished she had quit before she had the chance to die.

And maybe everyone else was really just waiting to see how long I would last. All those writers who wrote about Mama, all those guys on opposing teams, maybe even the guys on my own team, maybe even my brothers—maybe they were all waiting for me to fade away and become a memory. Like Mama.

Well, they wouldn't have to wait to find out. I'd pull the rug out from under all of them and pull the roof down on myself. I was in charge.

But I knew that the only way for me to fail right away was to tank, and I also knew that if I was going to tank convincingly, I needed to practice. It was probably pretty hard to boot a routine ground ball.

Everything started out fine. First of all, I was on time. And I was still mad.

"Good to see you, DiMarco," Coach Jameson greeted me as I jogged out to my place at shortstop.

I waved my glove in the air at Ross, who was sitting alone in the grandstand again. My one big fan.

Don't miss this! I wanted to shout to him. I'd give him something to write about.

Coach Jameson hit a couple of grounders to Cal Landry at second before giving me my first chance. Then he hit a completely routine, medium bouncing ball to short. I took a deep breath and booted that thing all the way back to home plate. The Red Hill players would have loved it, last Saturday. I laughed long and hard, in silence.

"Oh, man!" Cal shrieked. "Look whose feet grew in the night!" The whole team cracked up. Perfect.

Coach Jameson shook his head and picked up the same ball. My footprint must have been all over it.

"This ball just got the best of you, DiMarco," he called out. "Now you got to teach it a lesson."

He swung low at the ball, sending it high into the air, a pretty ordinary pop fly to short. I camped under it and opened my glove, closing it a second before the ball was about to land in the webbing. It caromed off the back of the glove instead, bouncing into the outfield.

"Sorry!" I said loudly. I saw Ross jump to his feet, and something about the way he stood there let me know that at least one person did not believe I was sorry at all.

It was fun for a while, my introduction to the world of terrible baseball. But by the time I had made my tenth error in a row, no one was laughing anymore.

Cal edged over toward me from second base. "Come on, Ruth, get serious," he said in a low voice. He looked kind of scared, but at least he was looking at me. The rest of the team was studying the ground beneath them, kicking dirt or playing with their shoelaces.

Coach Jameson called Matt Paterson in from the sidelines. He handed the bat to Matt.

"Keep it going, Paterson," was all Coach said. Then he looked at me over at shortstop and pointed to the left-field fence. Time for some discipline.

I met Coach Jameson out in left field, in foul territory.

"What's up, Coach?" I asked, realizing I was pushing at his limits even as I said it.

"You want to go home now, DiMarco?" he demanded, his voice low. "I don't know what's going on here, but maybe you're better off at home until you get it out of your system."

"I'm okay, Coach," I said. "I just want to play baseball." My voice sounded high and squeaky and goofy—like the voice of something Coach might want to step on.

He shook his head. "Go home," he said. "We can't use you here today." He turned his back to me and started to walk away.

"But, Coach," I started to protest, and he whipped around fast before I could say another word.

"Go home." His words were hard. Then he put up his hand as if to stop himself. "I don't know, DiMarco," he said more gently. "I thought you loved this game. I thought you had more pride."

Coach didn't have to say another word. My stomach lurched as I climbed over the left-field fence and ran across the softball field bordering ours. I stopped in the nearby parking lot only when I realized that I did not want to go home.

I climbed up onto a parked station wagon and stood on the hood. I heaved my glove as far as I could and watched it bounce off somebody's blue pickup truck onto the pavement.

I looked down at the parking lot. The pavement was littered with broken glass and gravel and cigarette butts. I wanted to cry.

I jumped off the station wagon and ran after my glove, rescuing it from East Shore's pollution.

"So, you want to keep it after all," a voice said. I looked up at Ross standing in front of me. He was carrying a brand-new wooden baseball bat.

"I can't help it," I said, turning away from him. "I love the thing. I mean, it's my *glove*."

"Here," Ross said, holding out the bat. "I was going to give this to you to hit with during batting practice. I thought you might like to try a real major-league baseball bat instead of those aluminum clubs all you kids are playing with these days."

I handed my glove to Ross and took the bat. The wood was smooth and the bat felt heavy and solid. It was the finest baseball bat I had ever held.

"Why are you here?" I asked Ross. I stepped aside and took a few swings, as if I didn't really want an answer.

"I saw you run off, and I wanted to make sure you were okay," he said.

"No," I said. "In Maine. Why are you here in East Shore? Is it really just because of me?"

Ross slipped my glove onto his hand and punched the pocket.

"Nice glove," he said. He looked at me closely and smiled one of his real smiles. "I'm here to write a story about you," he explained. "And I wouldn't be here if you weren't a special baseball player. But I will admit that I was skeptical when your father pitched the idea, and I only took this assignment out of respect for him. I figured that at best I'd end up with a nice human-interest story about a girl who plays baseball with the boys. But now that I know you and have seen you play . . ."

Ross kept on talking, but I couldn't hear him. *When your father pitched the idea . . .*

It all made sense, sort of. If my father had been trying to make a living out on some lobster boat all summer, would *Sports Illustrated* really have sent a reporter to do a story about me? Not likely. It was because of my father. Ross was in East Shore because of my famous father.

I was suddenly aware of the silence. I didn't know if Ross had finished saying what he had to say or if he'd just stopped talking because he knew I had stopped listening.

"What is wrong with my father?" I asked, not sure whether my voice was a scream or a whisper.

"He loves you, Ruth," Ross said. "And he's proud of you, too, and he wants everybody to know it. He wants to celebrate you now—"

"Because there won't be anything to celebrate later," I interrupted. "He thinks it's over, doesn't he? He thinks this is as good as it gets, as good as *I* get."

"Ruth, you need to listen to me," Ross said. "This

story was your father's idea, but that ends his involvement. No disrespect intended, because Tony DiMarco is a great writer, but that's where his expertise ends."

Ross stopped talking and stared off at the field, watching my teammates practice.

"You know," he said after a moment, "your father only wants what's best for you, but he has no idea how good you really are. He doesn't get it. He can't see past his little girl."

I didn't know whether to laugh or cry. I hugged Ross's bat tightly, cradling it like a baby, and then I sat right down in the middle of the parking lot, right down on the torn-up pavement. I didn't even check for broken glass.

Ross sat right down next to me. He didn't check for broken glass, either.

"Nice bat, isn't it?" he said. "Maybe someday you'll play all the time with bats like this. Maybe someday bats like this will be made just for you, with your signature on them."

I looked at Ross. For the second time since I had met him, I didn't know whether I wanted to hug him or hit him. I placed the bat gently in his lap.

"Maybe someday," I said. I sighed and was surprised to hear the catch in my breathing. "My mother's dead, you know."

Ross nodded. "I know. I'm sorry."

"She died eight years ago."

"I know."

I turned to Ross, my voice growing louder. "Then why does it feel like she died yesterday?"

He didn't answer, and I was glad. I took my glove back from him and stood up. I turned toward the baseball field and watched my teammates run the bases. Base-running drills. Coach Jameson only had us do those before big games.

Ross got up and stood next to me. "What happened out there today?" he asked.

I shrugged. "I played like somebody whose mother died." Ross didn't say anything. I looked up at him. "You wouldn't understand," I said. "I mean, were you any good at baseball when you were my age?"

"I was okay," Ross said. "Nothing like you."

"Yeah? Well, do you know how hard it is to drop a fly ball?" I asked. "Do you know how hard it is to drop a fly ball when you know that feeling of the ball buried deep in the web of your glove is coming and you just *love* that feeling? And then you drop it anyway? Do you know how hard that is?"

Ross stared at me, but I couldn't stop myself.

"And you know what else?" I continued. "Do you know how hard it is to scoop up a ground ball and bring that ball back behind your ear and your arm is ready to throw a bullet to first and you *love* throwing bullets to first, but then you let that ball sail three feet over the first baseman's head? Do you know how hard that is?"

Ross put his hand on my shoulder. "Ruth . . . Ruth," he said, shaking me slightly as if I was asleep. "Do you have any idea how good you are? Do *you* get it?"

I watched my teammates gather together on the infield grass for an impromptu team meeting. Coach Jameson and Coach Dillon stood before them, talking about the game, talking about the team, maybe even talking about me.

"I feel it," I said slowly. "You know, I remember something Ellie's mom once said about some book she was reading—that the author could really make the words sing. Well, that's how I feel about baseball sometimes. Like I can really make this game sing."

Ross was staring into the distance, toward the field, but I wasn't sure whether he was really looking at anything.

"I want to see you play in that game on Friday," he said. "The real you. No more of this kicking the ball around stuff." He turned to me and smiled. "You know, Ruth," he said, "I've followed baseball all my life and covered the game professionally for more than ten years . . . I deserve it, don't you think? Let me hear you sing."

Chapter 10

Thursday morning. The day before the big game. Two days after the DiMarco family blowup. One day after the attempted tank. I slipped into my bathing suit, pulled on a T-shirt, grabbed a towel and a chocolate-chip granola bar, and flew out of the house. The beach and Ellie were about all I could handle.

No one was there when I arrived. I stepped over the short rock wall that marked where the parking lot ended and the beach began. I had just buried my toes in the still-cool morning sand when I heard a rhythmic, creaking, totally un-beach-like noise.

I turned around and there was Ellie, pulling a loaded little-kid's red wagon behind her.

"I had the best idea last night," she announced. "We are going to discover our creative selves right here on this beach."

"*Now* what have you been reading?" I asked.

"*Psychology Today,*" Ellie said. "My mother just started subscribing."

"*Psychology Today,*" I echoed. "Maybe they'll come and do an article about me next week."

Ellie looked at me for a moment before her eyes got wide and her whole face broke into a great big smile.

"You?" Ellie was practically spitting, but she was also laughing. "You know, Ruth, your ego is enormous. If *Psychology Today* was coming to East Shore, you would be a mere speck in my psychologically fascinating shadow."

"You're just jealous," I said, sticking my nose in the air, "because I'm more screwed up than you are." I danced around Ellie on my toes, kicking my legs up high like a really bad ballet dancer.

Ellie joined in, out-dancing and out-weirding me completely.

"Look at us, world!" Ellie shouted. "Who cares about *Psychology Today*? We're ready for *Vogue*!"

She jumped on my back and we both collapsed into the sand. Ellie rolled over and over, laughing and kicking until she was covered in dried seaweed and beach dirt. I was laughing, too, but more quietly, just because I was happy to be with my best friend.

Ellie sat up suddenly and hugged her knees.

"But you know, Ruth," she said, pausing to catch her breath, "if we were ever to be in *Vogue* for real, it would have to be some kind of special issue. Like 'Feminists in *Vogue*' or something." She grinned as if she couldn't wait for the opportunity.

I stretched out on the sand, lying flat on my back, studying the cloudless sky.

"If it was a special feminist issue," I said, "I don't think I'd even be invited to be in it."

"Oh, come on! Are you kidding?" Ellie kicked sand at me, pretending to be angry. "You'd probably be on the front cover."

I flopped over on my stomach and folded my arms into a pillow in front of me, resting my head on them. I rolled my eyes and looked up at Ellie.

"But lately I keep thinking how much easier life would be if I was a boy," I explained. "That's terrible, isn't it? Not exactly feminist."

It was Ellie's turn to study the sky. She looked away from me but then turned back again before speaking.

"Of course it would be easier, Ruth," she said finally. "I mean, did you ever hear anyone say they wished they could throw like a girl? I know it's hard. Even for you. Perfect as you are."

I frowned. "It's weird, though. I don't hear them say it, but I know a lot of guys on my team wish they *could* throw like me. And hit. And field."

"Exactly," Ellie said, grinning. "See? You don't really need to hear them say it. Feminists know the truth."

"I guess you're right." I couldn't disagree. Sometimes Ellie made everything seem so simple.

"And do you want to know what else is true, Ruth?" she continued. "I'm not a feminist just because of my mother. Sure, she gives me stuff to read and everything, but she's not the real reason. I'm a feminist because of *you*."

My vision blurred from sudden tears as I lifted myself up off the sand. I crawled over to the wagon on my hands and knees, suddenly ready to begin whatever it was Ellie wanted us to do.

"Do I even want to know what's in here?" I called out.

Ellie leaped to her feet and was at my side in a second.

"This," she said, waving her arms all around, "is everything we need to create our beach mural."

"Beach mural?" I wasn't so sure about this idea. "Ellie, we can't paint on the sand. They'll ban us from the beach for life."

"I know," Ellie said. "Too bad, huh? But that's why I brought yards of newsprint."

"It'll blow away," I said, as if I was talking to a two-year-old.

Ellie pointed to a burlap sack in the wagon.

"Rocks," she said.

The next few minutes were amazing.

Ellie could really move when she wanted to. She had that newsprint spread out all over the beach faster than a major-league grounds crew can cover the infield in a sudden downpour. And the rocks were strategically placed at various corners in order to maximize the painting space while still holding down the mural. Ellie had obviously spent a lot of time planning this project. The least I could do was give it a try.

"Here," Ellie said, shoving a large paintbrush into my hands. "You go first. The paints are in the wagon."

There were four large pots of paint in the wagon. I checked out the colors: black, purple, some sort of aqua, and a screaming pink—not exactly primary colors, but then again, Ellie was not exactly the primary colors type.

"Hey, Ellie," I said. "How are we supposed to paint in the center of the mural?"

"We walk on it," she said.

"But won't we step in the paint and get footprints everywhere?"

"Ruth," Ellie said, totally serious. "Footprints are extremely cool."

I plunged my brush into the purple paint, ready to attack the mural.

"Um, Ellie? One more question," I said. "What am I supposed to paint?"

Ellie looked at me and sighed as if I was truly beyond hope. "Anything you want," she said. "Whatever makes you happy."

I jumped onto the newsprint, dragging my paintbrush in a big, wild loop. I painted a crisscross pattern at the top of the loop, then some stitches, then a wide, circular bottom. I stopped to examine my work.

It looks exactly like nothing, I thought, feeling safe.

Ellie appeared next to me. She studied my painting closely. "Great baseball glove," she said. "Extremely cool."

"It is not a baseball glove, Ellie," I lied.

"Of course it is," she said, pushing me gently. "Come on. Let's paint."

I watched Ellie dip her brush into the pink pot. She paused for a moment before taking off running, covering the mural with pink brushstrokes and purple footprints. She ran back and forth to the wagon, changing colors often, stopping only when she needed to catch her breath.

Finally Ellie stood still in the middle of the mural. Then she turned around slowly in small circles, checking her work. She was sweaty and flushed, and she was smiling.

"Well," she said, gesturing around her. "What do you think?"

I didn't know what I thought. I didn't even know what I was looking at.

"I don't know what it is," I admitted, "but it looks really creative."

Ellie walked toward me, leaving a trail of multicolored footprints behind her. She looked entirely pleased with herself.

"It's you, Ruth," she said. "It's you playing baseball."

I took a step backward, off the newsprint and onto the sand.

"It is not," I said softly.

"Can't you see yourself?" Ellie asked, stepping backward so that she was standing alongside me. She pointed at my purple glove. "Look," she said. "There's your glove. And those wild pink streaks over there? That's your hair. And there? The black part? Those are your legs, charging in on a ground ball to short."

And there, I said to myself, the aqua part over there. *That is my face.*

"I'm smiling, aren't I?" I said out loud.

Ellie nodded. "You're grinning your aqua face off."

I looked at her. "But I thought you were supposed to paint something that made you happy."

Ellie stepped back out onto the mural. "I did," she said, and she opened her arms as if she was part of the mural herself.

I didn't know what to say. I curled my toes into the sand. We were both silent as Ellie danced around on the mural, making new footprints.

"Ruth," she said, as if she had never stopped talking, "when I see you out there, playing better than all those boys . . . it's like, some kind of pride, you know? I just want to stand on my seat and shout 'That's Ruth DiMarco! She's a girl and she's my best friend!' "

I jumped out to the center of the mural, with Ellie.

"Let's paint some more," I said. "This mural is the best weird idea you ever had."

Ellie dashed off to the wagon to get more paint. I followed her slowly, looking down at the mural beneath my feet. I liked my wild pink hair and long black legs and happy aqua face. I liked making footprints and I loved my best friend and I knew I was smiling, for real.

Only Ellie could have turned a mural into a mirror.

Saturday afternoon
    —bottom of the 6th, runner on second, two outs, Red Hill 2, East Shore 5

I know just where I am.

I'm at Mitchell Community Park standing at shortstop and leaning a little toward second base, ready to hold the runner on, and I'm wearing my East Shore All-Stars uniform and cap, and we're about to win another game and I know I've been an important part of everything.

I know I should be feeling really good right now, happy and proud and excited, and as soon as we get the third out I should feel all the tension rush out of my body, and I should throw my glove into the air like everybody else will and run off the field into Coach Jameson's arms. I should. The funny thing is, I probably will do all of those things, but I won't feel like it. I'll be acting.

Why am I out here?

Do I love this game? Do I love what it is, its history and its . . . future?

Will I always dream about baseball?

The batter connects lightly on the next pitch and lofts a lazy pop fly to short center field. I backpedal quickly and am standing under the ball as it practically floats out of the sky. I reach out and grab it, squeezing it tightly in the webbing of my glove.

I want to hug my glove with the ball in it, close to my chest. I want to be happy.

Cal throws his glove high into the air and bounces over to me, slapping me on the back.

"And the ball game is over!" he shouts, just like a TV announcer.

But I don't want the ball game to be over. I want it to go into extra innings, I want to play in the dark, I want to keep playing when the sun rises in the morning. I want to drop the ball and keep on dropping it so that there will never be a third out.

The ball game cannot be over; I cannot let it end. If I do, I know that it will be the second great loss of my life.

Chapter 11

"Can I walk with you?" Lou asked. "Or are you going with Ellie?"

I hadn't even seen him, standing there on the porch. I hadn't seen much of Lou at all for the past three days, although I wasn't exactly looking for him myself, either. But there he was Friday afternoon, an hour before the big game, waiting for me.

"Ellie's going with her mother," I said. "So, you're coming to my game after all," I added, too quickly. I tucked my glove under my arm and fingered the buttons on my uniform.

"Of course I'm coming to your game," Lou said. "I'll walk with you to the field, okay?"

It was a beautiful afternoon. It was the kind of afternoon that can make you think baseball was invented to be played in eastern Maine in the summertime. The thermometer on our porch had read 75 degrees, but in East Shore that always meant it was warmer in the sun and cooler when an ocean breeze came your way.

I licked my lips and tasted salt. The breeze was strong enough so the ball would tend to sail but not so strong that anyone would get a home run who didn't deserve it.

We took the long way to the ballpark, walking along streets and sidewalks and staying out of people's backyards. Lou said he was getting too old to be seen sneaking behind someone's azaleas. I wondered why he wanted to walk with me. He didn't seem to have anything real to say.

My brother waited until we were on Mitchell Road in full view of the field before he decided to speak.

"You miss Mama, don't you?" he said, looking at me.

I stared across the street, watching my teammates arrive in groups of two and three. I had been playing with most of those guys since T-ball. They didn't need a *Sports Illustrated* article to know all about me.

"You know," Lou continued, "I never knew you could miss someone you never had."

"I had Mama," I said. "I'm allowed to miss her."

Lou shrugged. "You were three when she died, Ruth. No way you had her like Joe and I did."

"So what?" I said, feeling my face flush as my stomach turned to ice. "She was my mother, too."

"I know," Lou said. "I know that now. I mean, I always knew it, but only in the past couple of days have I really known it."

I faked a laugh. "I don't think you know what you know," I said. "You're not even making sense."

"Ruth, just this morning I was looking at you in your uniform sitting there at the kitchen table, and for the very first time, I said to myself, 'Her mother is dead, too.' " Lou turned away from me, looking toward the field. "And that's cool, you know? I never even thought about it before, but suddenly I feel like I know you. We've got something in common."

"We've always had something in common," I said.

Lou nodded. "I'm sorry, Baby Ruth," he said as he reached out to me.

At first I wasn't quite sure what he was trying to do. Then I let him pull me close as I wrapped my arms around him. I couldn't remember the last time we had hugged or even whether we had ever hugged before.

Suddenly I laughed, startling even myself. Lou pulled back to look at me.

"What's so funny?" he asked. He smiled as if he wasn't sure whether I was laughing with him or at him.

"I don't know," I said. "I just thought of something strange." I searched Lou's face for a possible clue, but he was waiting for me to say more.

"Poopy kiss," I gasped, breaking out laughing again. "What does that even mean?"

Lou didn't laugh.

"It's . . . it's what you used to say when I would kiss you good night . . . when we were little." My brother looked at me closely. "Do you remember, Ruth?" he asked. "Joe would kiss you first, and then I would, and then you would always laugh and say 'poopy kiss.' And then Mama would laugh and say 'No, no, Sofia, you mean sweety kiss,' and she would kiss me all over my face. Don't you remember, Ruthie?" Lou spoke rapidly, excited by the memory. His eyes were shining.

I was stunned.

"Mama called me Sofia?" I asked softly.

"All the time." Lou reached out to hug me again. "I can't believe I forgot all about that," he said.

"Sofia?" I said again, my voice muffled by my brother's shoulder. "Sofia."

Josh Callahan appeared across Mitchell Road, hanging out as if he was waiting for someone. The guy had great timing. I wondered if Lou would ever hug me in public again.

"Hey, DiMarcos!" Josh called out. "Are you getting over here or what?"

Lou gave me one last squeeze before letting go quickly and running his hands through his hair.

We crossed the street and Josh held out his open palm to me. I slapped it hard. Josh smiled and groaned.

"Big game today, Ruthie," he said. "You got to take this team to the regionals. Take on the big boys in Bangor."

"No problem," I said, because it wasn't. I wasn't worried about Sacksport or Bangor or any other team from anywhere. I was more concerned about who was going to be out there in the stands, watching me play baseball, listening to me sing, and who would be wondering why.

Chapter 12

The Sacksport team was different in a funny sort of way. They stared at me. They knew all about me and everything, that was no secret. But most of the guys on other teams would avert their eyes every time I walked by; they dealt with me by ignoring me. The Sacksport guys just stared. Cal Landry and some of the other guys on my team made this big show of staring back at them, but I couldn't be bothered. It didn't seem important.

When both teams had finished pregame warm-ups, Coach Jameson came up to me with a bat in his hand.

"What do you say?" he asked. "Want to shag a few? Put on a little show for these guys before the game?"

I looked over at the Sacksport dugout. They were all staring, even the coaches.

"No," I said. "I'm not putting on a show for anyone. They can wait for the game to begin."

Coach nodded. "That's fine," he said. "But tell me, DiMarco. Are you ready to play today?"

"More than that, Coach," I said. "I *need* to play today." I stared at the field. I knew I needed to play a game so special that it would let last Saturday go.

Coach looked at me for a moment. Then he smiled, but his face was still serious. "I fear for the Sacksport All-Stars," he said. "But don't forget to have fun."

Fun. He actually said *fun.* I wanted to laugh or maybe cry or maybe just give Coach J. a kiss in appreciation of his way with words.

The stands filled up just as the game was about to begin. I jogged out to the infield alongside Cal.

"Give it all you got, Ruth," he said. "We really need this one today." The poor guy actually sounded worried.

"It's okay, Cal," I said. I slapped my glove against his. "I'm here. I'm all here."

I scanned the stands quickly. Ellie was there, and so was her mother. Dad was there. Joe and Lou and Josh were all sitting together. Ross was there.

Ross waved at me. I waved back. Sam Beals had just about finished his final warm-up pitches when suddenly I knew I had to talk to Ross. I had something to say that was so important, I could not believe I had never said it to him before.

"Let's go, East Shore!" someone bellowed from the stands. Too late. Sam was going into his windup, for real. I would have to find Ross after the game.

Sam struck out Sacksport's lead-off hitter, and then I felt an old familiar feeling wash over me. The blinders came up and blocked out everything until the only thing in my line of vision was a small white ball with red stitching, and I knew I could do anything. I was about to enter the zone, and it felt like a dream, a dream that I knew I could make come true.

Hit it to me. I want the ball.

The next hitter seemed to understand. He hit a fairly routine ground ball to short, but I charged it so hard I was practically at the pitcher's mound when I scooped it up and side-armed it to first. Two outs.

I slapped Sam's hand on my way back to short. I kicked at the dirt around me and adjusted my cap as I checked out the next batter. Short legs, squat body, square head. He didn't look like a ground-ball hitter, but I could hope. I still wanted the ball.

The square guy had a pretty swing, and I got to see it

three times as he went down on three straight pitches. I dashed off the field and into the dugout. I grabbed my favorite bat out of the rack and held it over my head, stretching out my shoulders. I was up third in the order. Babe Ruth batted third. So did Joe DiMaggio. And so did Ruth DiMarco, all the time.

And Sofia. Sofia loves baseball, too.

I almost dropped the bat. I grabbed it quickly, just before it hit the ground, and brought it up to my chest, holding it close, hugging it. I stood there, still and listening, until it was my turn in the on-deck cage.

There were two outs when I dug in at the plate. I took the first pitch, a hard fastball right down the middle. I glanced at the pitcher, who was staring at me. Good. The guy had decent stuff. He came right back at me with another heater.

I slammed it. I was actually thinking about going to the opposite field, but I got all of it and drove the ball in almost a straight line deep to left center. It collided with the left-field fence and bounced right back to their center fielder. He grabbed it, whirled, and threw, but by that time I was standing on second, adjusting my helmet. The crowd cheered loudly, like one unified sound with no distinct voices. And then I heard something, or someone, or maybe I felt it.

Such a smart girl! Such a big smile!

My head popped up fast and I looked around. I didn't

know who I expected to see. Cal had just stepped up to the plate, and everyone else was looking at him. I peered down at Coach Dillon in the third-base coach's box, but he wasn't giving me any sign, to stay or to go. He trusted my judgment, that meant. I trusted my judgment, too. I took off on the next pitch.

The Sacksport catcher rifled the ball to third, but I had surprise on my side. I dove headfirst and was hugging the bag when the third baseman slapped his glove down on my arm. I called time and jumped to my feet, brushing off my pants as the crowd roared.

Sofia, beautiful girl. You make Mama so proud!

I held my breath as I recognized the image that flew through my mind. I was standing at the top of our living room stairs, looking down at the bottom in wonder, because I had just climbed up alone for the first time in my life. I was so proud I was ready to burst, and then I saw a smile, my mother's smile, telling me it was good to be proud.

And I *was* proud. I was proud to have climbed the stairs, and I was proud to have stolen third base, and I was proud to be playing shortstop for the East Shore All-Stars, playing for the right to go to Bangor, and then Portland, and then maybe all the way to Williamsport, Pennsylvania, to represent Maine at the Little League World Series. I was proud that the sky was the limit.

Look at me, Mama!

I looked down again, down at my feet, back down

the living room stairs, and there was my mother, still smiling.

And then I smiled, too, standing right there on third base, because I knew I wasn't hearing voices. I was remembering. I had Mama, too.

Chapter 13

We won the game, 1–0.

I homered to dead center field my second time up, and that was the difference. Sam Beals pitched a beautiful game, and so did their guy, for that matter, even though he walked me intentionally my last two times at bat. But Sam had his ground-ball pitches going, and I had lots of chances at short—so many, in fact, that I had a hard time remembering the last time I had been in that good a groove. I felt great about the way I played, and I knew I wanted to feel that way again and again, forever.

My brothers mobbed me before I could even get off the field. They didn't say much, they just kept thumping me on the head and back and every now and then throwing an arm around me in something that almost felt like a hug.

It was Josh Callahan who wouldn't shut up.

"Way to go, Ruthie," he shouted as I slapped his hand. "I just got one thing to tell you," he continued, leaning forward so that I wouldn't miss a word. "Watch out for the intentional walk. Good pitchers will do that to you, thinking they can shut down the rest of the team. You're going to have to learn to cross the plate and knock that pitch into the opposite field."

I caught Joe rolling his eyes. "Right, Callahan," my brother said, "whatever you say. We all live for your advice."

"Hey, it's what I do best," Josh said. "I'm a true student of the game. I don't expect to make it all the way to the majors, so I've got two fallback positions. Coach or sportswriter."

Sportswriter. I grabbed Joe's arm hard. "Where's Ross?" I asked. "I really need to talk to him right away."

"His plane leaves out of Portland tonight so he had to go get his bags and everything together," Joe explained. "But he did say he'd stop by the house for a few minutes this afternoon."

"I really need to talk to him," I said again.

"Don't worry, he'll wait for you. I think he wants to talk to you, too." Joe leaned down close to whisper into my ear. "I think there's someone else you really need to talk to even more."

I looked up and there was Dad, hanging in the background, looking as if he wasn't sure whether he was in the right place at the right time.

"I'm supposed to walk home with Ellie," I whispered back to Joe.

"I'll talk to Ellie," he said. "She'll understand." Joe gave me a look that told me I didn't have a choice. Of course Ellie would understand. That wasn't the problem.

I looked at my father again, and he smiled. "Hey, Dad," I called out. "You want to walk home?"

It was amazing how everyone left us alone. I saw Lou steer Josh in the opposite direction. Joe was turning on the charm with Ellie and her mother, and from the way Ellie was looking at him, I knew she wasn't about to miss walking home with me at all. Cal waved and blew me a kiss before taking off with Sam and some other guys on the team. Good guys. Buddies.

Dad was no fool; he knew what was going on, too. He smiled again. I smiled back, almost out of habit, because I knew it would make him happy.

We walked slowly, although I couldn't be sure who was setting the pace. The afternoon breeze had picked up, promising a cool, clear evening. I wasn't ready to say anything, and it was a relief when Dad spoke first.

"You played beautifully today, Babe," he said. "You can't imagine how proud I am."

That was a nice thing for Dad to say, but it wasn't what I wanted to hear.

"The whole game, I saw Mama," I said. I did not look at my father, but I could feel him flinch.

"I didn't even think I had any memories of her at all," I continued, "but the whole game, I saw her and heard her voice, too. At least I think so. I remembered the words. I remembered the feelings." I paused for a moment as my voice became softer. "I heard Mama calling me Sofia."

Dad stared straight ahead. "I'm glad," he murmured. I wanted him to say more.

"Mama would have thought I could play in the major leagues," I said.

Dad stopped and turned toward me, but I took a couple more steps forward before turning back.

"Maybe you can," Dad said. "There's always a first. Maybe you're the one."

I could not believe what I was hearing. I could not believe that my father would lie to me.

"But you don't think I can," I said, my voice quivering. I wished I had the strength to scream. "You think all of my talent is a waste because I'm a girl. I heard you before the game last Saturday, talking to the other parents. You said it's all a shame. I heard you."

Dad stared at me. "I thought you were mad at me because of your mother, and the articles—"

I cut him off cold. "This has got nothing to do with

Mama," I said. My voice was almost a whisper, and I gave up on the idea of screaming.

"Ruth, I was wrong," Dad said quickly, putting his hands on my shoulders. "I didn't know what I was saying. I don't know what I was thinking. I just don't want you to get hurt. Your talent is . . . it's special. It's a beautiful thing."

"No, it's not!" I said to my own astonishment. And then I heard my voice growing stronger and louder as I listened to words I had never even heard in my mind: "I can't play in the major leagues. I'll never play in the major leagues."

And then I couldn't stop, and I knew I was crying, and I knew my father was not ready for any of this, but I could not wait for him any longer.

"I always thought that was part of the plan, playing in the major leagues," I said, struggling to keep my voice even. "I always thought I could. I mean, I always knew there were never any women, but I didn't think it mattered. I just figured people didn't have choices a long time ago, that it all sort of happened by accident, that it was all a mistake."

Dad pulled me closer to him, and I wrapped my arms around his waist. I waited for my breathing to return to normal.

"I never thought about it much before," I said. "I never let myself think about it much before. And now I don't know what to think."

Dad kissed the top of my head.

"Ruth," he said, "I spend a lot of time examining the past. Your mother was the one who looked forward." He nestled his face in my hair. "And remember this," he said softly. "You already know the truth. Mama would have thought you could play in the major leagues."

I loosened my hold around Dad's waist and leaned back so that I could see his face.

"It *is* all about Mama," I said. "I know that."

Dad nodded. "Ask me anything."

"Did Mama love me?"

Dad was not surprised by this question. He nodded again and smiled. "Yes," he answered, confirming what I already knew.

"Let's walk," I said, slipping my hand into his.

We walked together in silence until we rounded the corner at the top of our street and our house came into view. Ross's rental car was parked in the driveway. And not far beyond our house, on the opposite side of the street, I could see Ellie's house.

Dad squeezed my hand. "It's nice walking home with my daughter," he said.

I stopped walking. Dad turned to me, still smiling.

"Did I love Mama?" I asked. "Did I smile when she came into my room in the morning? When I saw her . . . was I happy?"

Dad stopped smiling. "Yes," he said, his voice fading. "Yes, yes, yes."

"Was I happy?" I repeated.

Dad nodded. "You were happy," he said. He turned away from me, toward our house. His eyelashes glistened in the afternoon light. "And then you forgot. You forgot how to be happy."

I held Dad's hand tightly. "Help me remember," I said.

Chapter 14

Ross met us on the front porch. He held his hand out to Dad.

"It's been a pleasure," he said.

Dad gave me a quick kiss. "I'll leave you alone to say good-bye."

I was still holding Dad's hand, and I did not want to let go. "No," I said. "Stay."

"I hate to leave so quickly," Ross said to me. "I'll give you fair warning before the article is published." He smiled and wrinkled up his nose. "This is going to be a first for me, you know. More of an essay than a typical article—kind of a Tony DiMarco piece, actually. Must be something in the air up here." He shrugged. "Anyway, maybe I'll finally get my Pulitzer."

"Not before me," Dad cut in. They both laughed. I was glad they liked each other.

"There's just one thing I want to tell you," I said to Ross. "I mean, my dad's a journalist so I know better than to tell you how to write your article, but there's just this one thing."

Ross smiled again. "Go right ahead."

"Say I love baseball," I said. "Get that in there. Say I love baseball. Because it's the truth."

"I know," Ross said. He reached out and messed up my hair, and that was okay. I knew he didn't know what else to do.

He started down the porch steps, heading back to his life and the rest of the world. Then he stopped and turned around again.

"You know, I'll be waiting for you," he said. "Waiting and looking."

"Where do you expect to find me?" I asked.

"All the way. The sports story of the twenty-first century." Ross looked at my father and grinned. "And it's mine," he added. "All mine. People will say I discovered her."

Dad pulled me closer to him. "You can have the story," he said to Ross. "I've got everything else."

Ross waved as he strode to his car. He opened the door and climbed in.

"Hey, Ross!" I shouted suddenly. "One more question." I ran down the porch steps to the driveway and leaned in the car window. "When you were a kid, growing up, when you were my age . . . did you ever wish you were a girl?"

Ross started to laugh but stopped quickly.

"No. Never." He shook his head. "I'm sorry." He placed both of his hands on the steering wheel. He did not look at me when he spoke.

"But maybe I should have," he said. "All this time, maybe I should have been wishing I knew how to play like a girl."

Friday afternoon

Lou has just dried the last dish from supper when he tosses the towel onto the counter and turns to Dad and Joe and me.

"Let's go out back," he says, "before it gets too dark."

It's been a long time since we've all been out back to play, and it seems like the best idea in the world.

Joe and Lou are out the door first, then Dad, and then me. I watch my brothers slip on their gloves and toss the ball back and forth, loose and easy. My brothers are natural athletes, just like me. My brothers love base-ball, just like me. I know that I love them. And I know that their mother is dead, too.

We play catch, the four of us, the way we used to, and before long it all gets competitive, the way it always did.

We throw the ball hard, releasing it quickly, trying to surprise one another. Dad and Joe and Lou are talking and laughing and boasting, but I am quiet and smiling.

It's getting dark, almost too dark to see, but I don't want to stop. I know that I am flushed and sweaty . . . and happy. I know that someone will drop the ball soon. And I know it won't be me.

ABOUT THE AUTHOR

Maria Testa grew up rooting for the New York Yankees in a baseball-loving family. She is the author of *Dancing Pink Flamingos and Other Stories* (an ALA Best Book for Young Adults), as well as several picture books. *Some Kind of Pride* is her first novel. Maria Testa lives in Portland, Maine, with her husband and two sons.